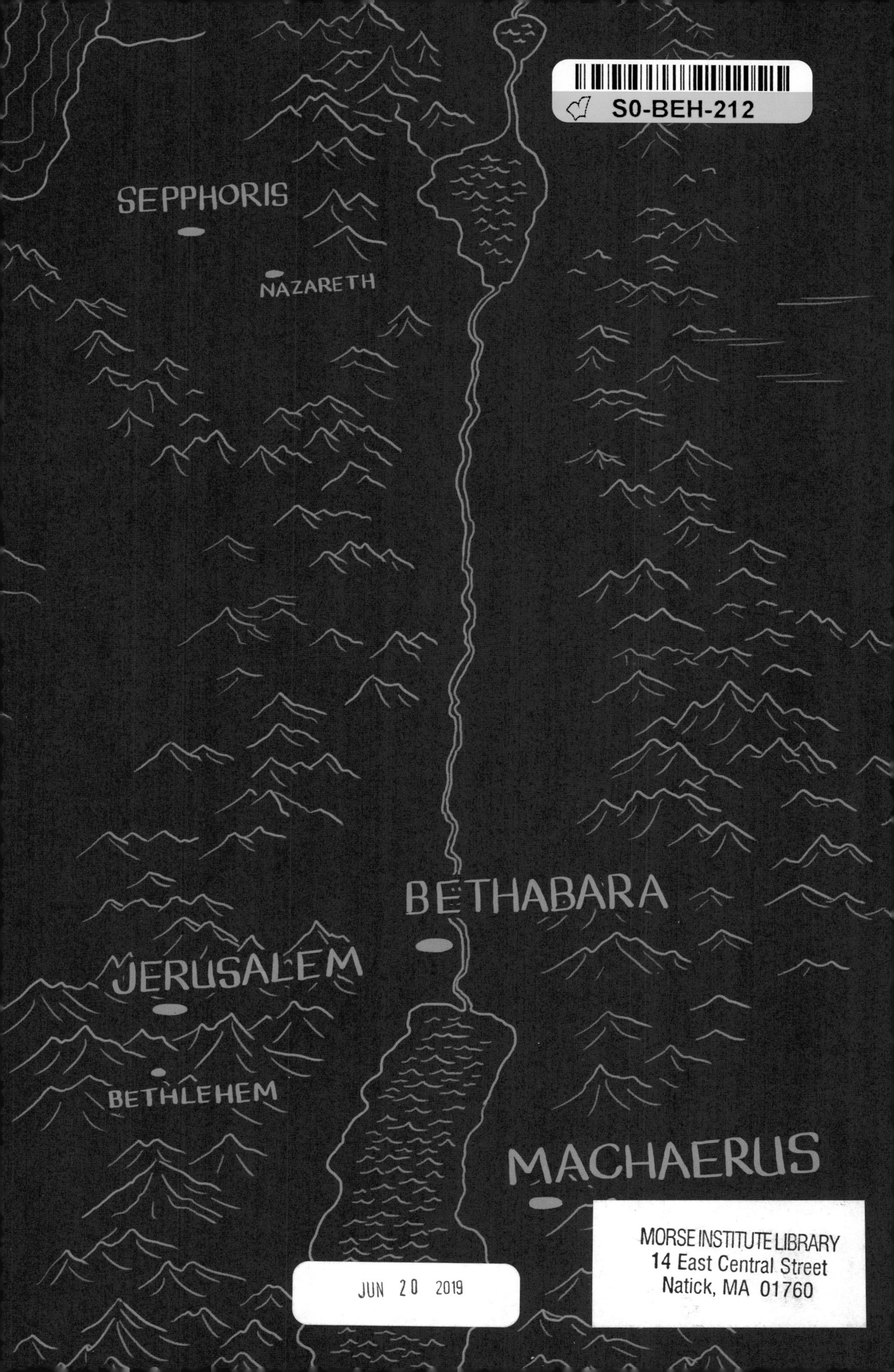
SEPPHORIS
NAZARETH
BETHABARA
JERUSALEM
BETHLEHEM
MACHAERUS

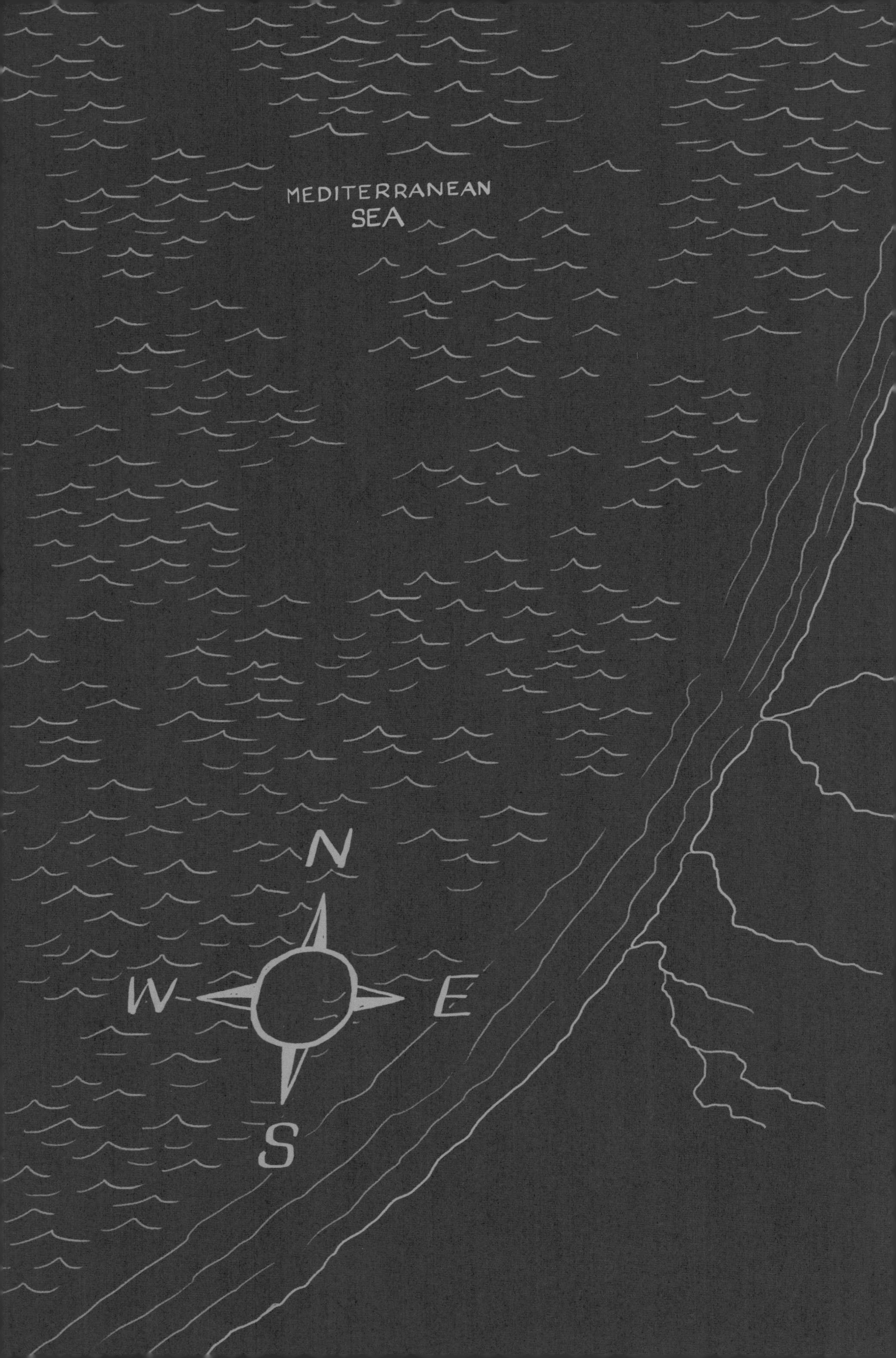
MEDITERRANEAN
SEA
N
W
E
S

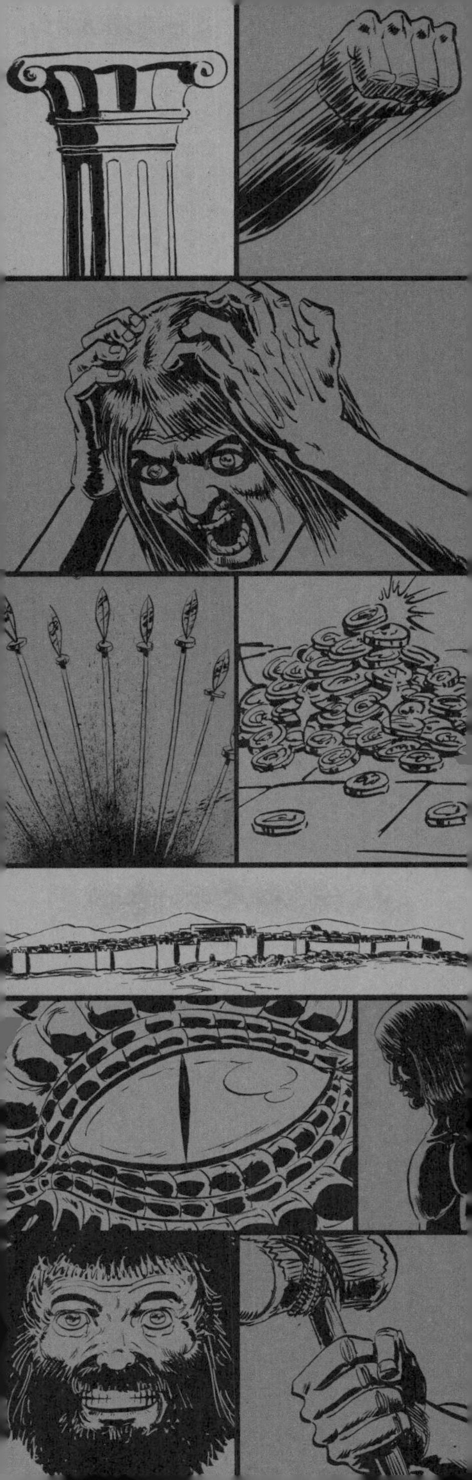

JESUS

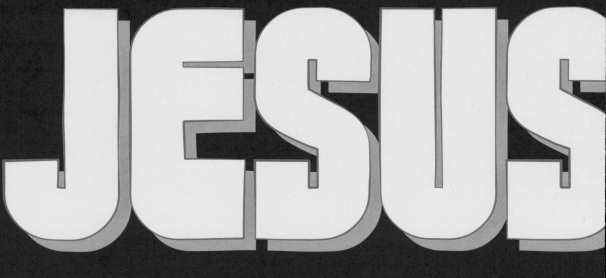

FREAK™

JESUSFREAK. First printing. March 2019. Published by Image Comics, Inc. Office of publication: 2701 NW Vaughn St., Suite 780, Portland, OR 97210. Copyright © 2019 Joe Casey & Benjamin Marra. All rights reserved. "Jesusfreak," its logos, and the likenesses of all characters herein are trademarks of Joe Casey & Benjamin Marra, unless otherwise noted. "Image" and the Image Comics logos are registered trademarks of Image Comics, Inc. No part of this publication may be reproduced or transmitted, in any form or by any means (except for short excerpts for journalistic or review purposes), without the express written permission of Joe Casey & Benjamin Marra, or Image Comics, Inc. All names, characters, events, and locales in this publication are entirely fictional. Any resemblance to actual persons (living or dead), events, or places, without satirical intent, is coincidental. Printed in the USA. For information regarding the CPSIA on this printed material call: 203-595-3636. For international rights, contact: foreignlicensing@imagecomics.com. ISBN: 978 1 5343 1174 9.

JOE CASEY
WRITER

BENJAMIN MARRA
ART

BRAD SIMPSON
COLOR

SONIA HARRIS
DESIGN

RUS WOOTON
LETTERS

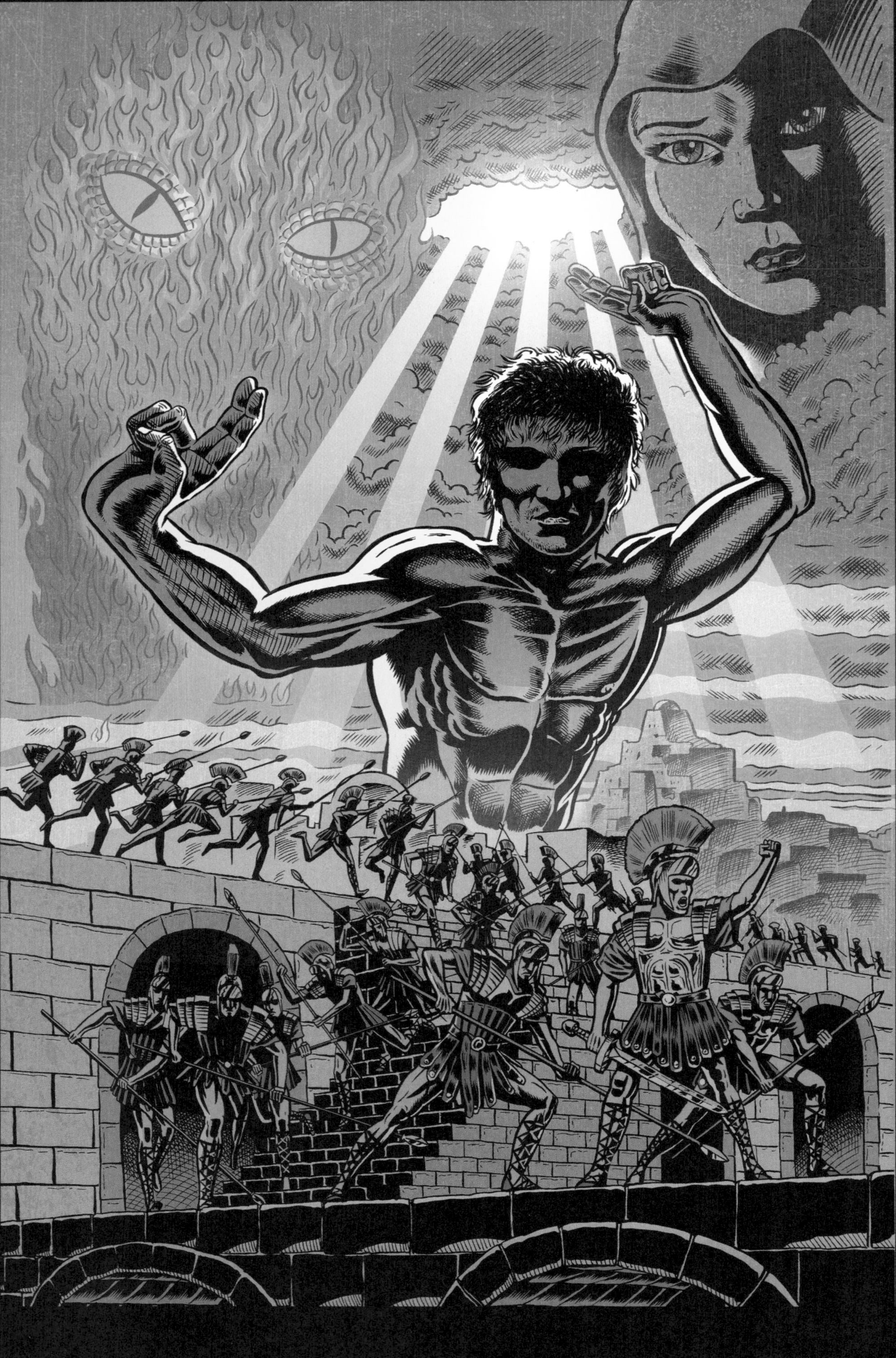

INTRODUCTION

Some say context is everything. So, full disclosure: This is not a religious story.

We thought it might be best to get that out of the way right at the top, so there's no misunderstanding whatsoever. We're not adapting the gospels. We're not espousing any particular point of view. We know the world is full of various religious persuasions and denominations. Your mileage may vary when it comes to their validity, but they're all out there and they're all a part of the vast mosaic that is the human race.

There are plenty of existing stories that deal with religion head-on. This is not one of them. Whatever you believe in your own life, more power to you. But this book is not meant to provide any deep, spiritual insight into anything of a religious nature. You want spiritual insight? Read the Bible. Read the Torah. Read the Quran or the Vedas or the Buddhist Sutras. Go to church. Go to temple. Meditate. Do whatever you need to do. But you're probably not going to find any answers here.

A fair bit of research went into the making of this book. Personally, that was part of the appeal for doing it. There are times when a research-heavy project is just what the creative mind desires and this was one of those times. But our book cannot -- and should not -- even be classified as "speculative fiction". Certainly for the sake of verisimilitude, we strove for a degree of historical accuracy, but not at the expense of accessibility.

For instance, in the text itself, we refer to our lead character -- by name -- as "Jesus", choosing not to call him by what was considered his more historically accurate name, "Y'shua" (of which "Jesus" is the English and Greek versions of the original Hebrew name). There was some back and forth on this one, but ultimately we chose accessibility. It's tough to have 100% certainty when it comes to details like this. It might be a bit of a gamble, but as comicbook creators, gambling is what we do.

Readers should also assume that the primary language being spoken -- by Jesus specifically -- is Jewish Palestinian Aramaic, the common language of Judea in the First Century. Some historians believe that Jesus also spoke Hebrew on occasion, but again, we felt like spotlighting these linguistic distinctions -- within the story itself -- would only end up obfuscating the intent of the story we've set out to tell. Again, accessibility bring a primary factor.

So, clearly, we're not here to be scholars. We're storytellers.

And, as storytellers, we try not to let anything get in the way of a good story. Certainly not "the truth", whatever that is in this particular instance. There are times when we lean pretty heavily into moments of pure symbolism. There are other times when we dive head-first into surrealism. Whether or not Jesus -- the man or the Christ -- even existed is completely irrelevant to the existence of JESUSFREAK. We're just here to put on a show.

We hope you enjoy it.

THE WORLD OF JESUSFREAK

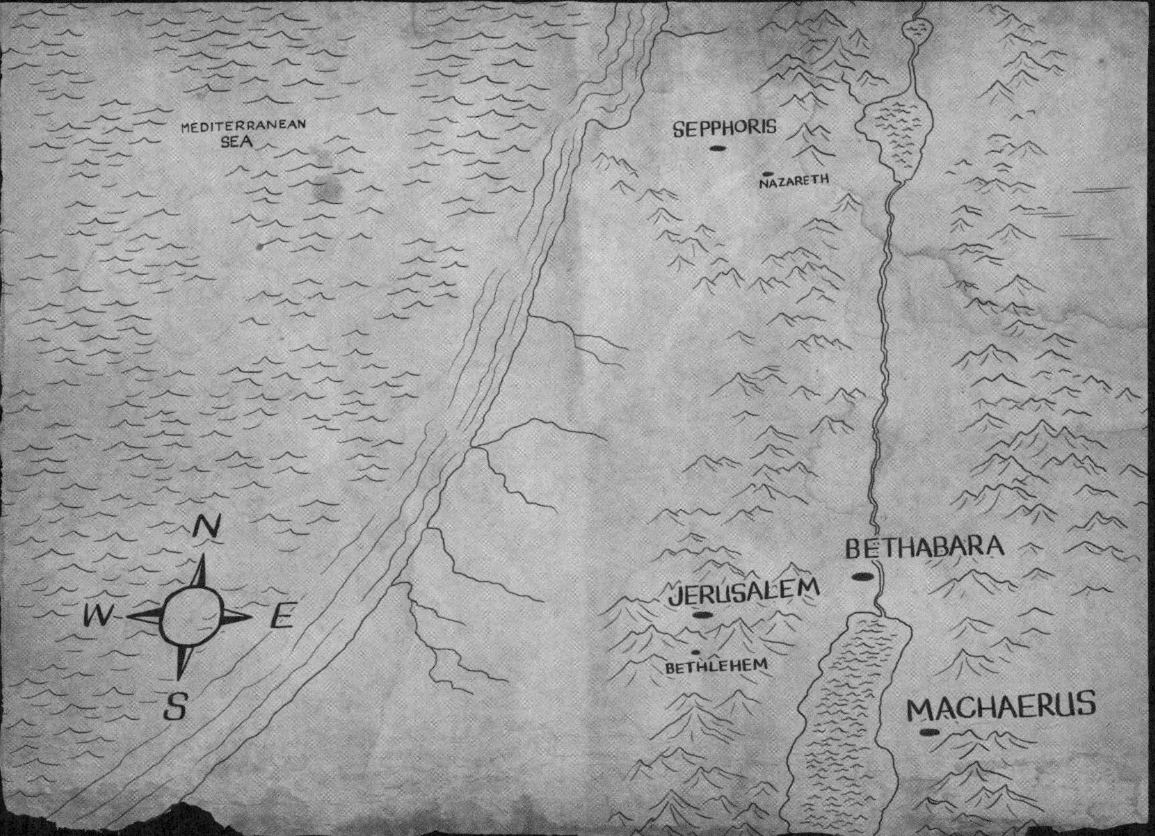
MEDITERRANEAN SEA
SEPPHORIS
NAZARETH
BETHABARA
JERUSALEM
BETHLEHEM
MACHAERUS
N
W
E
S

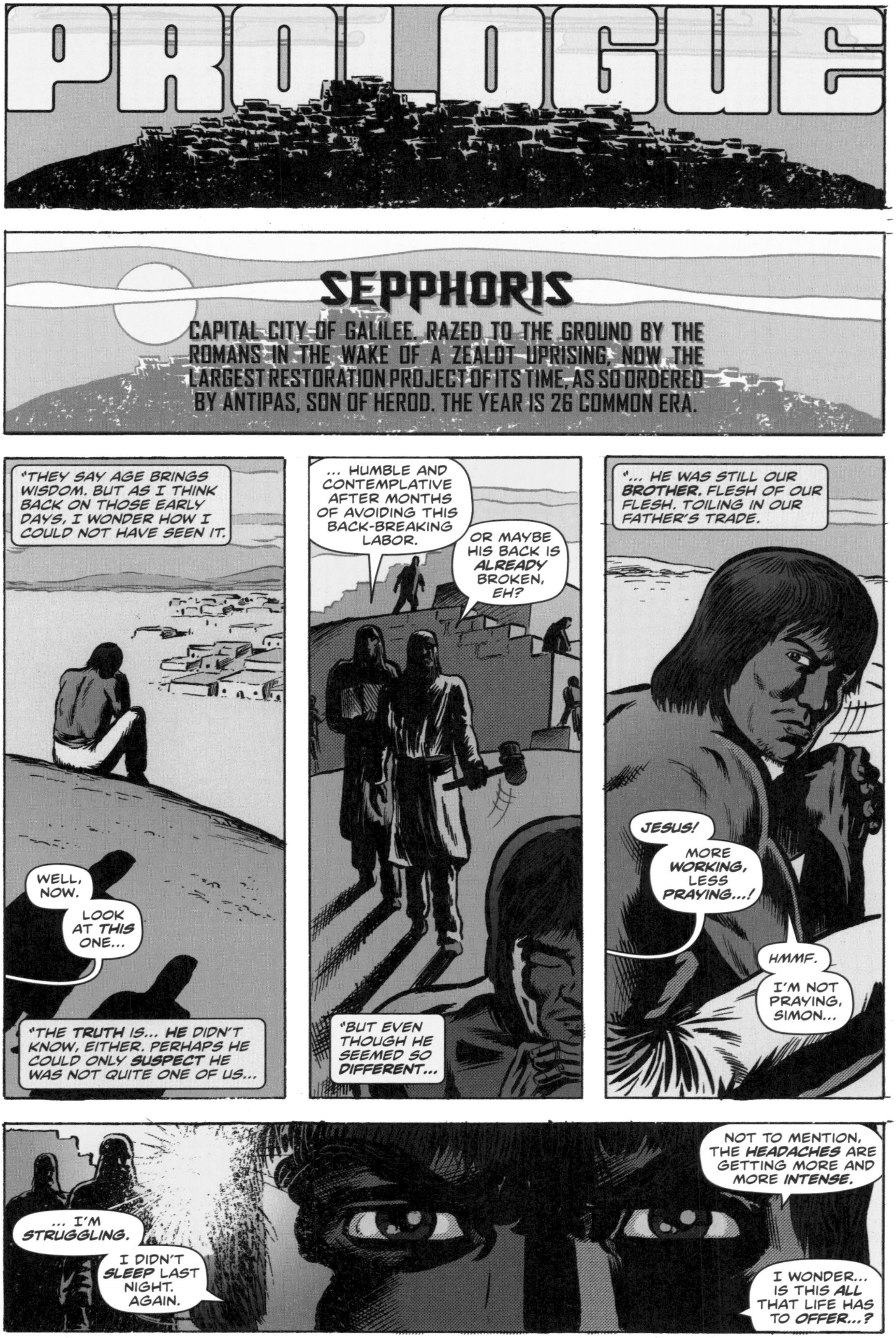
PROLOGUE
SEPPHORIS
CAPITAL CITY OF GALILEE, RAZED TO THE GROUND BY THE ROMANS IN THE WAKE OF A ZEALOT UPRISING, NOW THE LARGEST RESTORATION PROJECT OF ITS TIME, AS SO ORDERED BY ANTIPAS, SON OF HEROD. THE YEAR IS 26 COMMON ERA.
"THEY SAY AGE BRINGS WISDOM. BUT AS I THINK BACK ON THOSE EARLY DAYS, I WONDER HOW I COULD NOT HAVE SEEN IT.
WELL, NOW.
LOOK AT THIS ONE...
"THE TRUTH IS... HE DIDN'T KNOW, EITHER. PERHAPS HE COULD ONLY SUSPECT HE WAS NOT QUITE ONE OF US...
... HUMBLE AND CONTEMPLATIVE AFTER MONTHS OF AVOIDING THIS BACK-BREAKING LABOR.
OR MAYBE HIS BACK IS ALREADY BROKEN, EH?
"BUT EVEN THOUGH HE SEEMED SO DIFFERENT...
"... HE WAS STILL OUR BROTHER. FLESH OF OUR FLESH. TOILING IN OUR FATHER'S TRADE.
JESUS!
MORE WORKING, LESS PRAYING...!
HMMF.
I'M NOT PRAYING, SIMON...
... I'M STRUGGLING.
I DIDN'T SLEEP LAST NIGHT. AGAIN.
NOT TO MENTION, THE HEADACHES ARE GETTING MORE AND MORE INTENSE.
I WONDER... IS THIS ALL THAT LIFE HAS TO OFFER...?

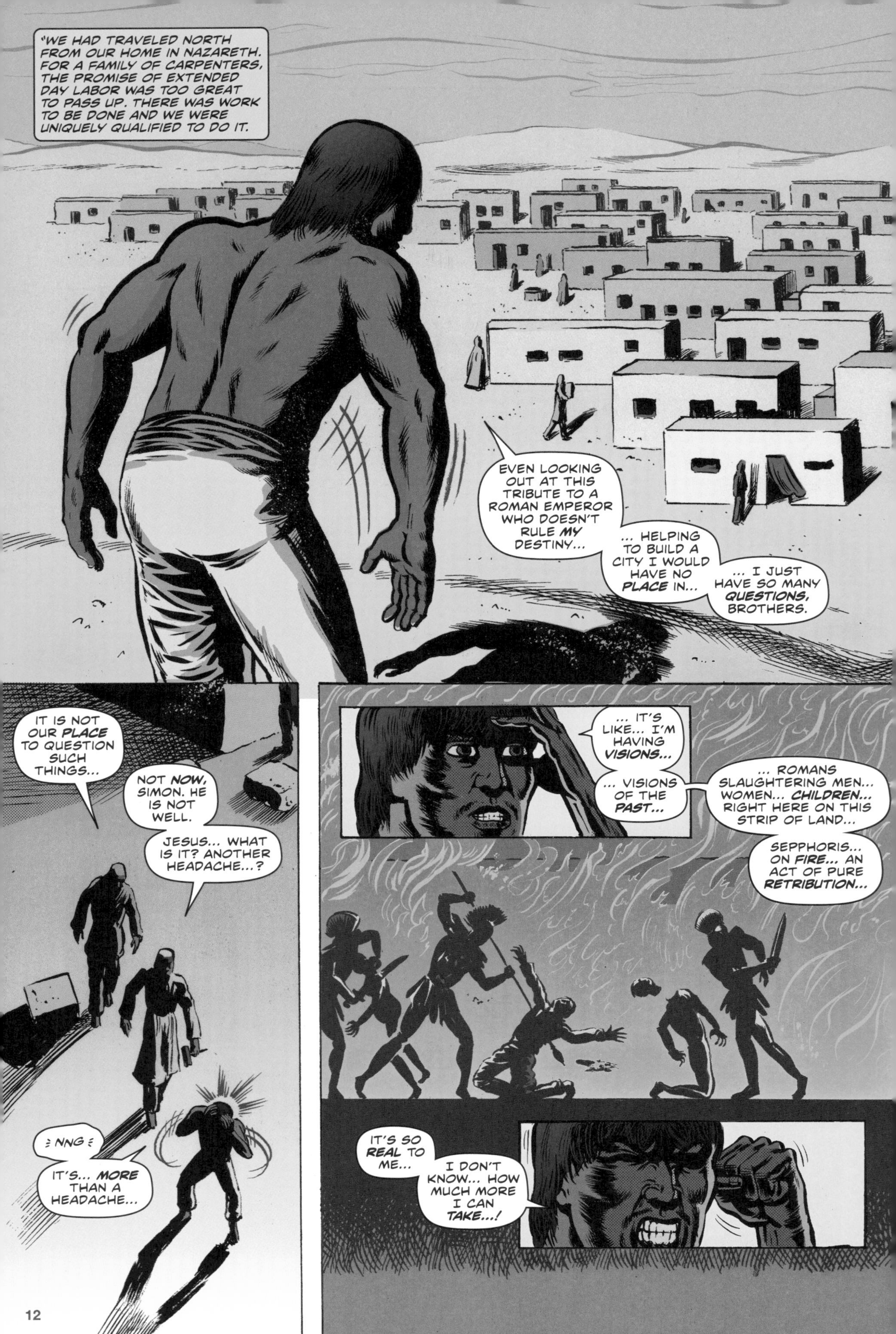
"WE HAD TRAVELED NORTH FROM OUR HOME IN NAZARETH. FOR A FAMILY OF CARPENTERS, THE PROMISE OF EXTENDED DAY LABOR WAS TOO GREAT TO PASS UP. THERE WAS WORK TO BE DONE AND WE WERE UNIQUELY QUALIFIED TO DO IT.
EVEN LOOKING OUT AT THIS TRIBUTE TO A ROMAN EMPEROR WHO DOESN'T RULE MY DESTINY...
... HELPING TO BUILD A CITY I WOULD HAVE NO PLACE IN...
... I JUST HAVE SO MANY QUESTIONS, BROTHERS.
IT IS NOT OUR PLACE TO QUESTION SUCH THINGS...
NOT NOW, SIMON. HE IS NOT WELL.
JESUS... WHAT IS IT? ANOTHER HEADACHE...?
NNG
IT'S... MORE THAN A HEADACHE...
... IT'S LIKE... I'M HAVING VISIONS...
... VISIONS OF THE PAST...
... ROMANS SLAUGHTERING MEN... WOMEN... CHILDREN... RIGHT HERE ON THIS STRIP OF LAND...
SEPPHORIS... ON FIRE... AN ACT OF PURE RETRIBUTION...
IT'S SO REAL TO ME...
I DON'T KNOW... HOW MUCH MORE I CAN TAKE...!

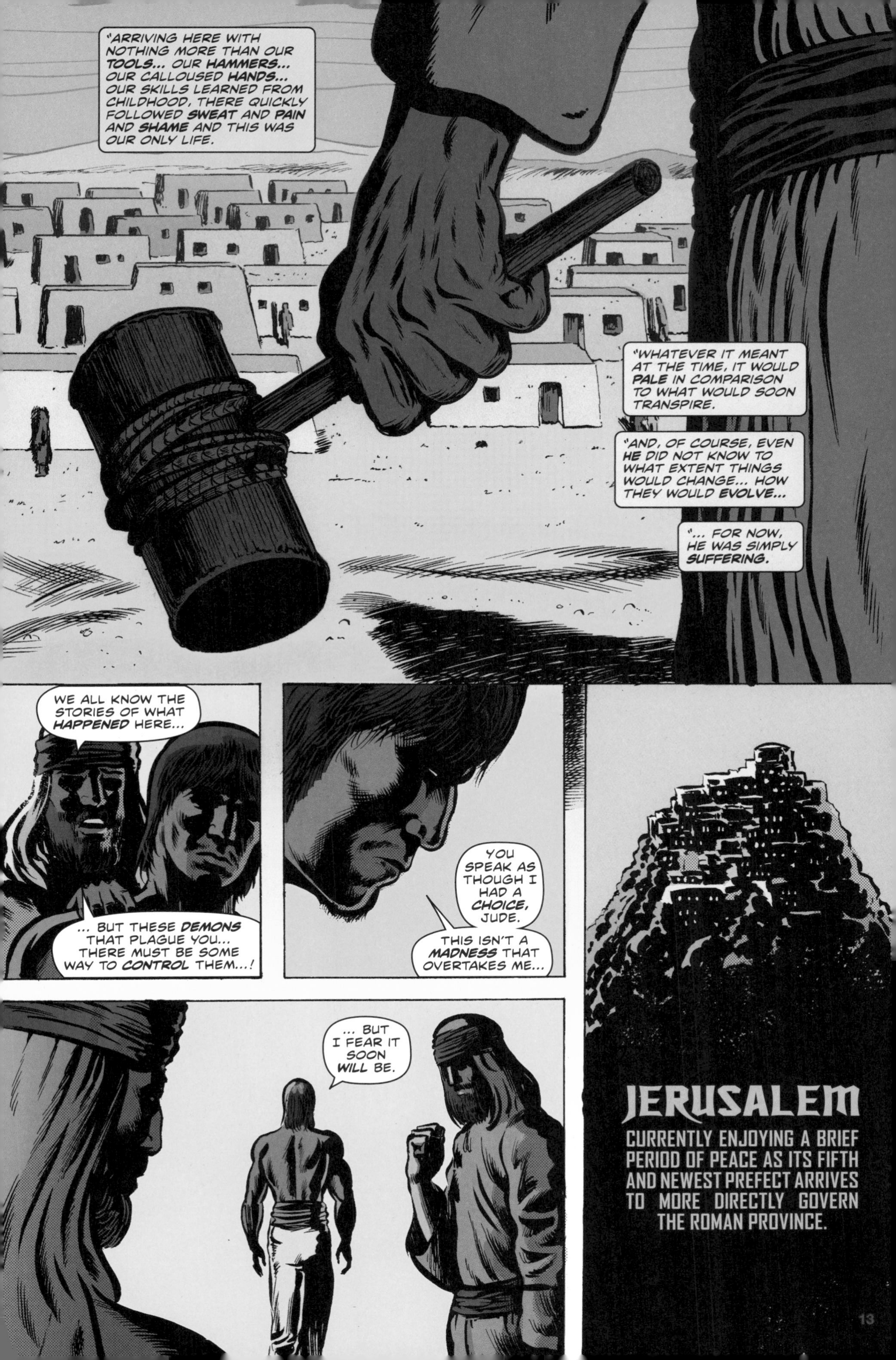
"ARRIVING HERE WITH NOTHING MORE THAN OUR TOOLS... OUR HAMMERS... OUR CALLOUSED HANDS... OUR SKILLS LEARNED FROM CHILDHOOD, THERE QUICKLY FOLLOWED SWEAT AND PAIN AND SHAME AND THIS WAS OUR ONLY LIFE.
"WHATEVER IT MEANT AT THE TIME, IT WOULD PALE IN COMPARISON TO WHAT WOULD SOON TRANSPIRE.
"AND, OF COURSE, EVEN HE DID NOT KNOW TO WHAT EXTENT THINGS WOULD CHANGE... HOW THEY WOULD EVOLVE...
"... FOR NOW, HE WAS SIMPLY SUFFERING.
WE ALL KNOW THE STORIES OF WHAT HAPPENED HERE...
... BUT THESE DEMONS THAT PLAGUE YOU... THERE MUST BE SOME WAY TO CONTROL THEM...!
YOU SPEAK AS THOUGH I HAD A CHOICE, JUDE.
THIS ISN'T A MADNESS THAT OVERTAKES ME...
... BUT I FEAR IT SOON WILL BE.
JERUSALEM
CURRENTLY ENJOYING A BRIEF PERIOD OF PEACE AS ITS FIFTH AND NEWEST PREFECT ARRIVES TO MORE DIRECTLY GOVERN THE ROMAN PROVINCE.

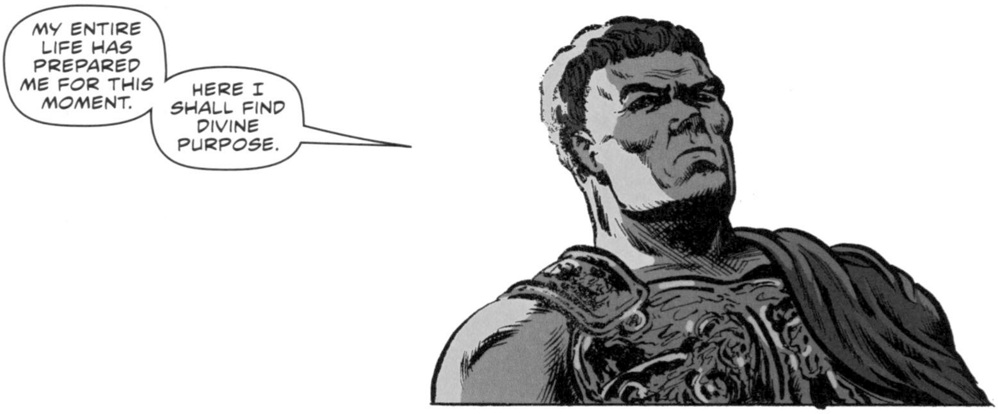
MY ENTIRE LIFE HAS PREPARED ME FOR THIS MOMENT.
HERE I SHALL FIND DIVINE PURPOSE.

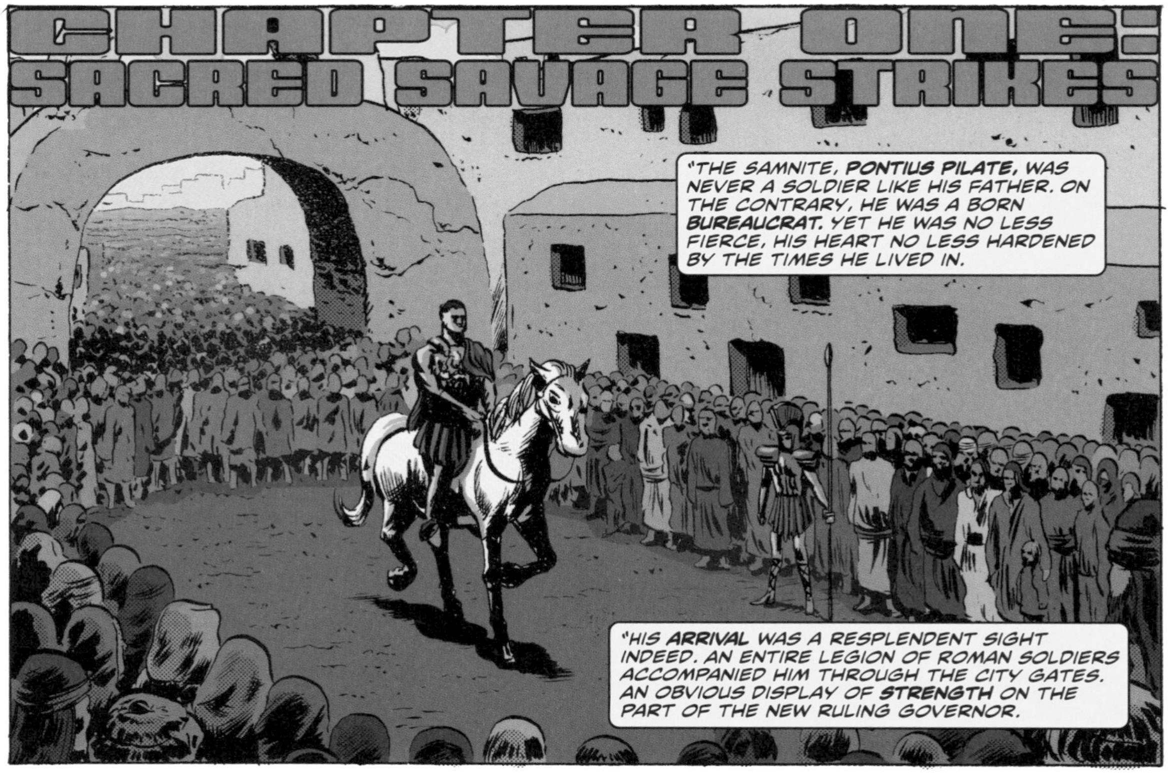
CHAPTER ONE: SACRED SAVAGE STRIKES
"THE SAMNITE, PONTIUS PILATE, WAS NEVER A SOLDIER LIKE HIS FATHER. ON THE CONTRARY, HE WAS A BORN BUREAUCRAT. YET HE WAS NO LESS FIERCE, HIS HEART NO LESS HARDENED BY THE TIMES HE LIVED IN.
"HIS ARRIVAL WAS A RESPLENDENT SIGHT INDEED. AN ENTIRE LEGION OF ROMAN SOLDIERS ACCOMPANIED HIM THROUGH THE CITY GATES. AN OBVIOUS DISPLAY OF STRENGTH ON THE PART OF THE NEW RULING GOVERNOR.

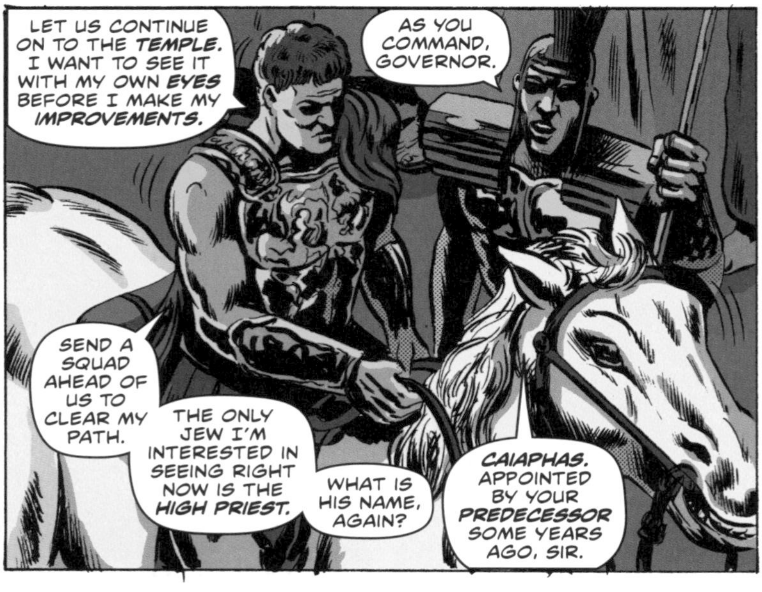
LET US CONTINUE ON TO THE TEMPLE. I WANT TO SEE IT WITH MY OWN EYES BEFORE I MAKE MY IMPROVEMENTS.
AS YOU COMMAND, GOVERNOR.
SEND A SQUAD AHEAD OF US TO CLEAR MY PATH.
THE ONLY JEW I'M INTERESTED IN SEEING RIGHT NOW IS THE HIGH PRIEST.
WHAT IS HIS NAME, AGAIN?
CAIAPHAS. APPOINTED BY YOUR PREDECESSOR SOME YEARS AGO, SIR.

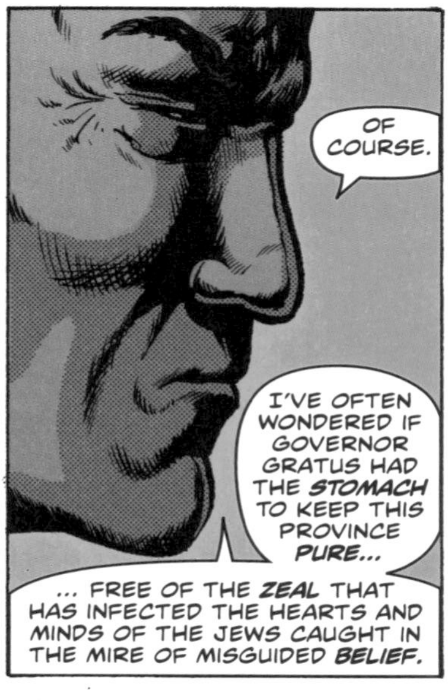
OF COURSE.
I'VE OFTEN WONDERED IF GOVERNOR GRATUS HAD THE STOMACH TO KEEP THIS PROVINCE PURE...
... FREE OF THE ZEAL THAT HAS INFECTED THE HEARTS AND MINDS OF THE JEWS CAUGHT IN THE MIRE OF MISGUIDED BELIEF.

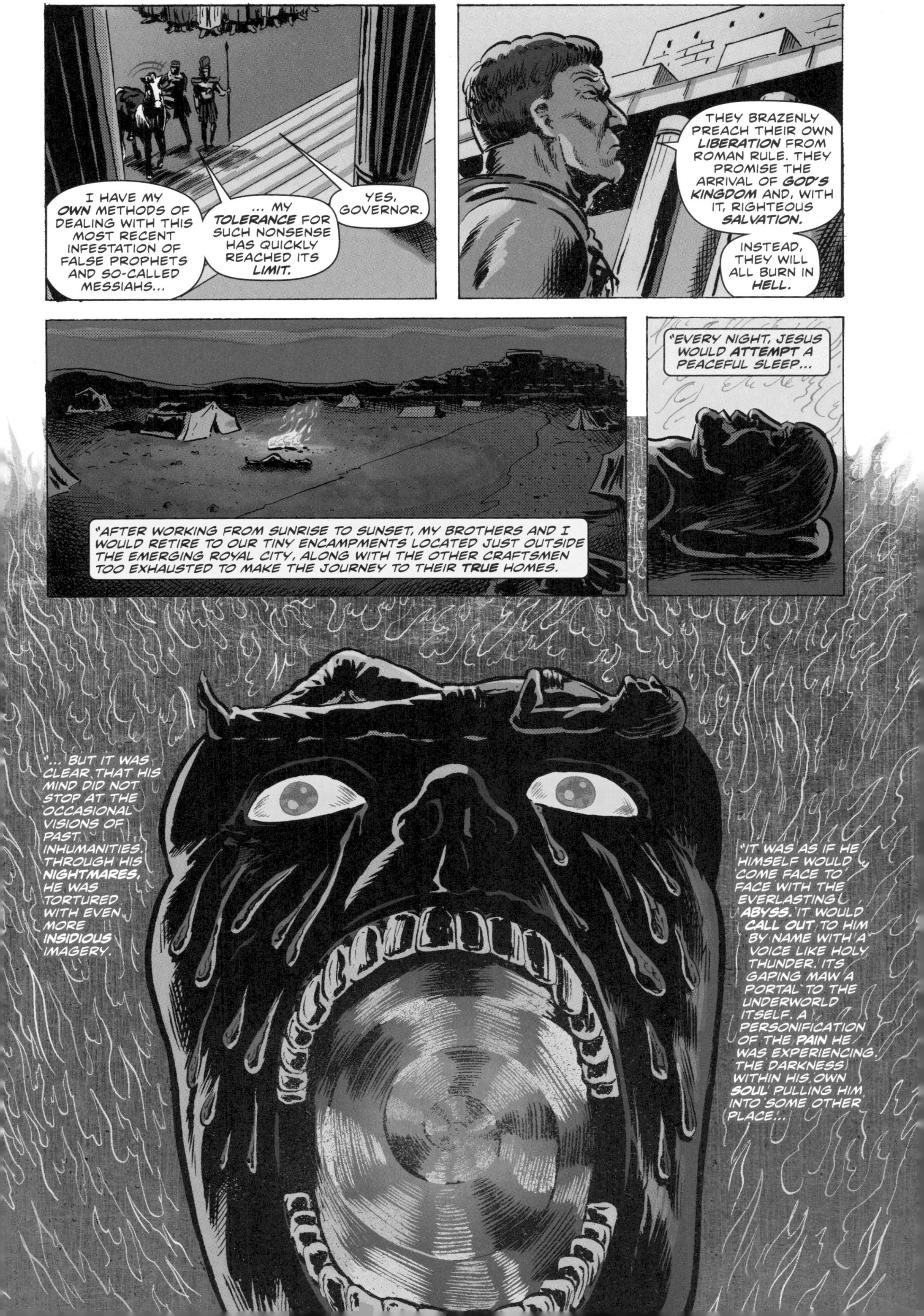
I HAVE MY **OWN** METHODS OF DEALING WITH THIS MOST RECENT INFESTATION OF FALSE PROPHETS AND SO-CALLED MESSIAHS...
... MY **TOLERANCE** FOR SUCH NONSENSE HAS QUICKLY REACHED ITS **LIMIT.**
YES, GOVERNOR.
THEY BRAZENLY PREACH THEIR OWN **LIBERATION** FROM ROMAN RULE. THEY PROMISE THE ARRIVAL OF **GOD'S KINGDOM** AND, WITH IT, RIGHTEOUS **SALVATION.**
INSTEAD, THEY WILL ALL BURN IN **HELL.**
"AFTER WORKING FROM SUNRISE TO SUNSET, MY BROTHERS AND I WOULD RETIRE TO OUR TINY ENCAMPMENTS LOCATED JUST OUTSIDE THE EMERGING ROYAL CITY, ALONG WITH THE OTHER CRAFTSMEN TOO EXHAUSTED TO MAKE THE JOURNEY TO THEIR **TRUE** HOMES.
"EVERY NIGHT, JESUS WOULD **ATTEMPT** A PEACEFUL SLEEP...
"... BUT IT WAS CLEAR THAT HIS MIND DID NOT STOP AT THE OCCASIONAL VISIONS OF PAST INHUMANITIES. THROUGH HIS **NIGHTMARES,** HE WAS TORTURED WITH EVEN MORE **INSIDIOUS** IMAGERY.
"IT WAS AS IF HE HIMSELF WOULD COME FACE TO FACE WITH THE EVERLASTING **ABYSS.** IT WOULD **CALL OUT** TO HIM BY NAME WITH A VOICE LIKE HOLY THUNDER. ITS GAPING MAW A PORTAL TO THE UNDERWORLD ITSELF. A PERSONIFICATION OF THE **PAIN** HE WAS EXPERIENCING. THE DARKNESS WITHIN HIS OWN **SOUL** PULLING HIM INTO SOME OTHER PLACE...

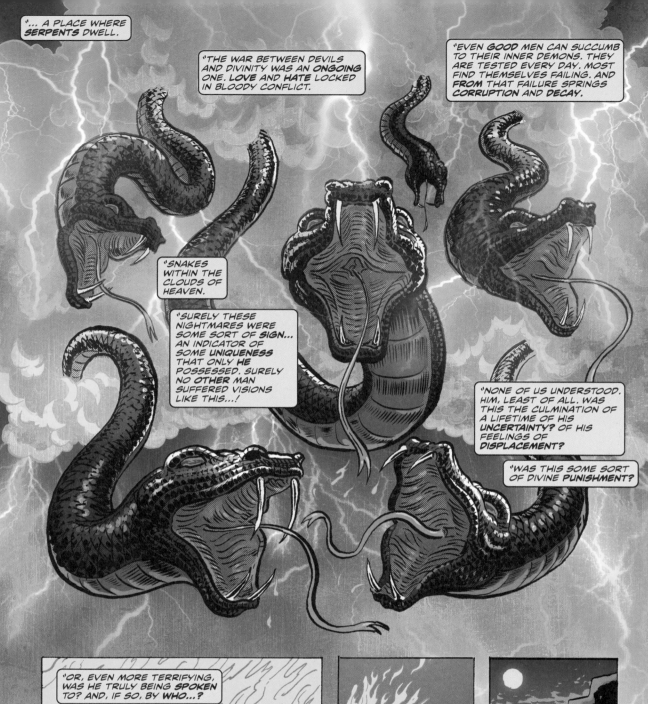

"... A PLACE WHERE SERPENTS DWELL.

"THE WAR BETWEEN DEVILS AND DIVINITY WAS AN ONGOING ONE. LOVE AND HATE LOCKED IN BLOODY CONFLICT.

"EVEN GOOD MEN CAN SUCCUMB TO THEIR INNER DEMONS. THEY ARE TESTED EVERY DAY. MOST FIND THEMSELVES FAILING. AND FROM THAT FAILURE SPRINGS CORRUPTION AND DECAY.

"SNAKES WITHIN THE CLOUDS OF HEAVEN.

"SURELY THESE NIGHTMARES WERE SOME SORT OF SIGN... AN INDICATOR OF SOME UNIQUENESS THAT ONLY HE POSSESSED. SURELY NO OTHER MAN SUFFERED VISIONS LIKE THIS...!

"NONE OF US UNDERSTOOD. HIM, LEAST OF ALL. WAS THIS THE CULMINATION OF A LIFETIME OF HIS UNCERTAINTY? OF HIS FEELINGS OF DISPLACEMENT?

"WAS THIS SOME SORT OF DIVINE PUNISHMENT?

"OR, EVEN MORE TERRIFYING, WAS HE TRULY BEING SPOKEN TO? AND, IF SO, BY WHO...?

UHH--!

N-NO...

"WHATEVER THESE NIGHTMARES WERE TRYING TO TELL HIM...

"... THEY DROVE HIM BACK TO THE CITY.

"BACK TO SEPPHORIS.

16

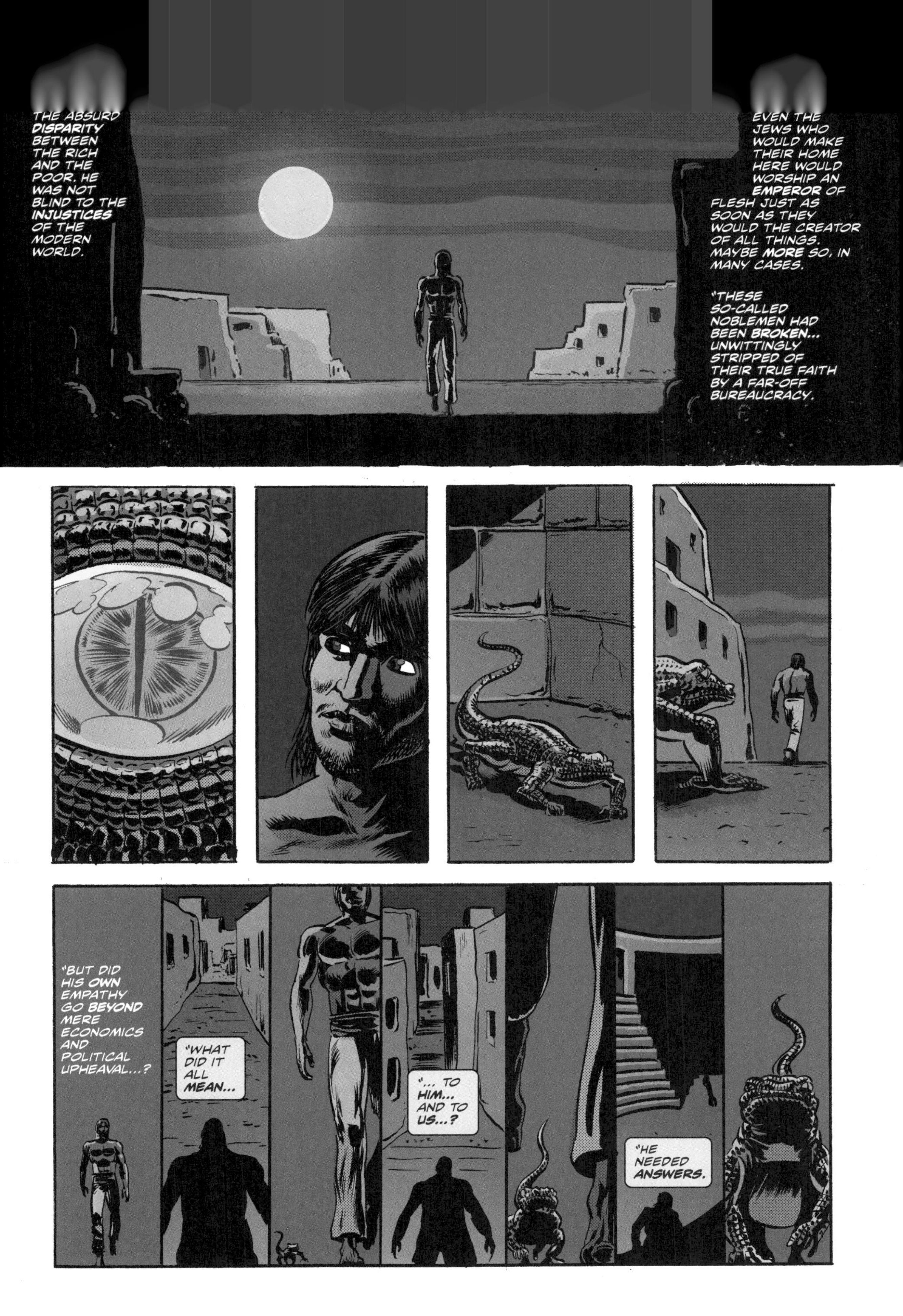
THE ABSURD DISPARITY BETWEEN THE RICH AND THE POOR. HE WAS NOT BLIND TO THE INJUSTICES OF THE MODERN WORLD.
EVEN THE JEWS WHO WOULD MAKE THEIR HOME HERE WOULD WORSHIP AN EMPEROR OF FLESH JUST AS SOON AS THEY WOULD THE CREATOR OF ALL THINGS. MAYBE MORE SO, IN MANY CASES.
"THESE SO-CALLED NOBLEMEN HAD BEEN BROKEN... UNWITTINGLY STRIPPED OF THEIR TRUE FAITH BY A FAR-OFF BUREAUCRACY.
"BUT DID HIS OWN EMPATHY GO BEYOND MERE ECONOMICS AND POLITICAL UPHEAVAL...?
"WHAT DID IT ALL MEAN...
"... TO HIM... AND TO US...?
"HE NEEDED ANSWERS.

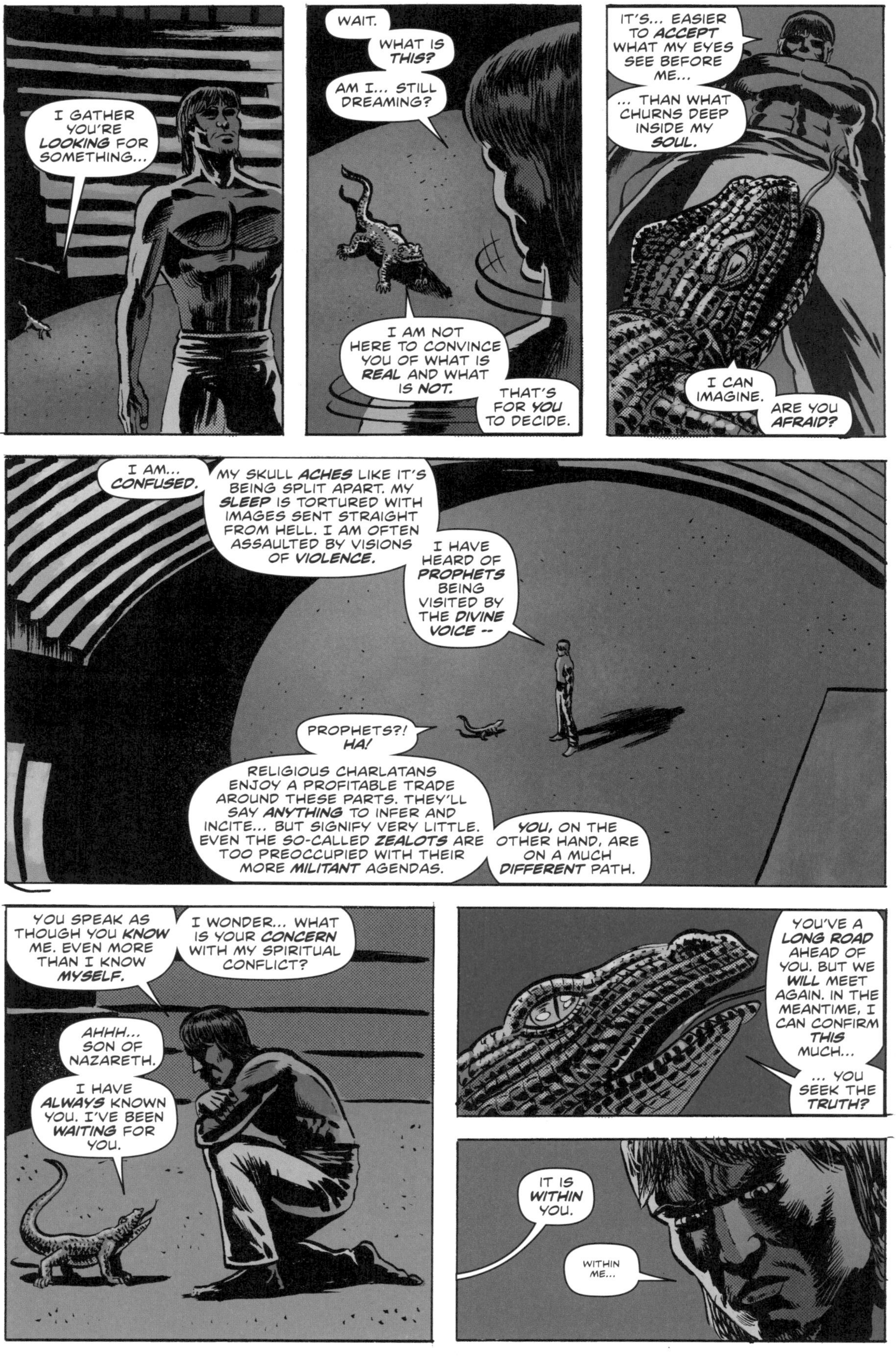
I GATHER YOU'RE LOOKING FOR SOMETHING...
WAIT.
WHAT IS THIS?
AM I... STILL DREAMING?
I AM NOT HERE TO CONVINCE YOU OF WHAT IS REAL AND WHAT IS NOT.
THAT'S FOR YOU TO DECIDE.
IT'S... EASIER TO ACCEPT WHAT MY EYES SEE BEFORE ME...
... THAN WHAT CHURNS DEEP INSIDE MY SOUL.
I CAN IMAGINE.
ARE YOU AFRAID?
I AM... CONFUSED.
MY SKULL ACHES LIKE IT'S BEING SPLIT APART. MY SLEEP IS TORTURED WITH IMAGES SENT STRAIGHT FROM HELL. I AM OFTEN ASSAULTED BY VISIONS OF VIOLENCE.
I HAVE HEARD OF PROPHETS BEING VISITED BY THE DIVINE VOICE --
PROPHETS?! HA!
RELIGIOUS CHARLATANS ENJOY A PROFITABLE TRADE AROUND THESE PARTS. THEY'LL SAY ANYTHING TO INFER AND INCITE... BUT SIGNIFY VERY LITTLE. EVEN THE SO-CALLED ZEALOTS ARE TOO PREOCCUPIED WITH THEIR MORE MILITANT AGENDAS.
YOU, ON THE OTHER HAND, ARE ON A MUCH DIFFERENT PATH.
YOU SPEAK AS THOUGH YOU KNOW ME. EVEN MORE THAN I KNOW MYSELF.
I WONDER... WHAT IS YOUR CONCERN WITH MY SPIRITUAL CONFLICT?
AHHH... SON OF NAZARETH.
I HAVE ALWAYS KNOWN YOU. I'VE BEEN WAITING FOR YOU.
YOU'VE A LONG ROAD AHEAD OF YOU. BUT WE WILL MEET AGAIN. IN THE MEANTIME, I CAN CONFIRM THIS MUCH...
... YOU SEEK THE TRUTH?
IT IS WITHIN YOU.
WITHIN ME...

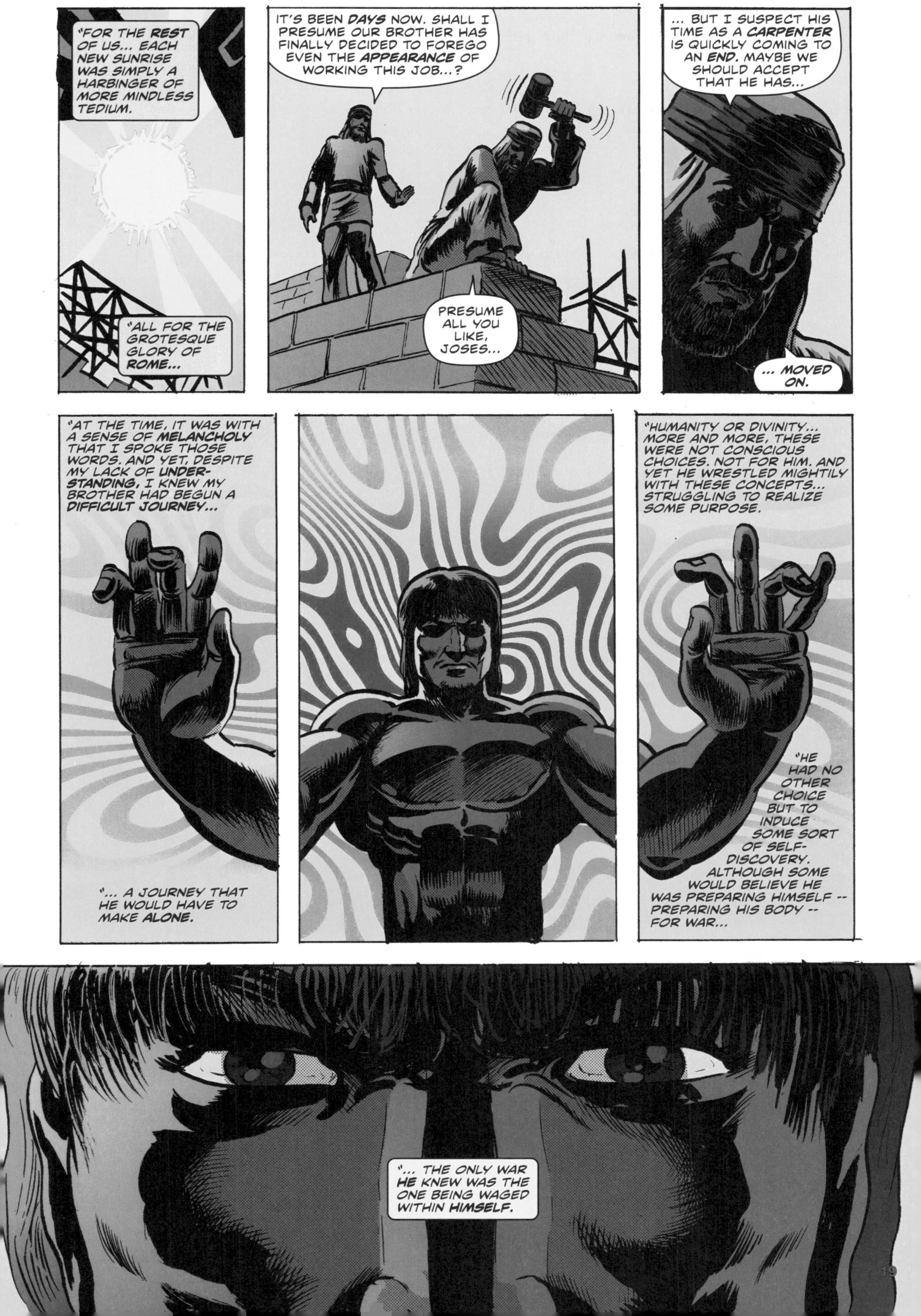
"FOR THE REST OF US... EACH NEW SUNRISE WAS SIMPLY A HARBINGER OF MORE MINDLESS TEDIUM.
"ALL FOR THE GROTESQUE GLORY OF ROME...
IT'S BEEN DAYS NOW. SHALL I PRESUME OUR BROTHER HAS FINALLY DECIDED TO FOREGO EVEN THE APPEARANCE OF WORKING THIS JOB...?
PRESUME ALL YOU LIKE, JOSES...
... BUT I SUSPECT HIS TIME AS A CARPENTER IS QUICKLY COMING TO AN END. MAYBE WE SHOULD ACCEPT THAT HE HAS...
... MOVED ON.
"AT THE TIME, IT WAS WITH A SENSE OF MELANCHOLY THAT I SPOKE THOSE WORDS. AND YET, DESPITE MY LACK OF UNDER-STANDING, I KNEW MY BROTHER HAD BEGUN A DIFFICULT JOURNEY...
"... A JOURNEY THAT HE WOULD HAVE TO MAKE ALONE.
"HUMANITY OR DIVINITY... MORE AND MORE, THESE WERE NOT CONSCIOUS CHOICES. NOT FOR HIM. AND YET HE WRESTLED MIGHTILY WITH THESE CONCEPTS... STRUGGLING TO REALIZE SOME PURPOSE.
"HE HAD NO OTHER CHOICE BUT TO INDUCE SOME SORT OF SELF-DISCOVERY. ALTHOUGH SOME WOULD BELIEVE HE WAS PREPARING HIMSELF -- PREPARING HIS BODY -- FOR WAR...
"... THE ONLY WAR HE KNEW WAS THE ONE BEING WAGED WITHIN HIMSELF.

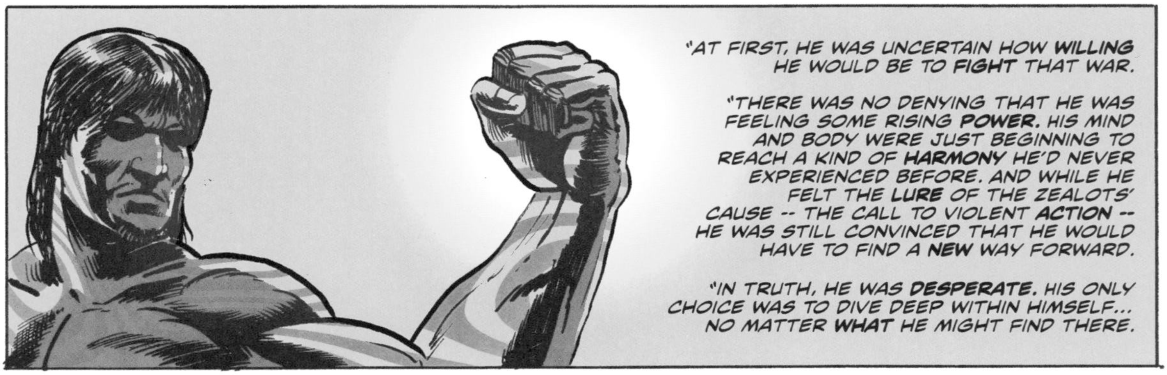
"AT FIRST, HE WAS UNCERTAIN HOW WILLING HE WOULD BE TO FIGHT THAT WAR.
"THERE WAS NO DENYING THAT HE WAS FEELING SOME RISING POWER. HIS MIND AND BODY WERE JUST BEGINNING TO REACH A KIND OF HARMONY HE'D NEVER EXPERIENCED BEFORE. AND WHILE HE FELT THE LURE OF THE ZEALOTS' CAUSE -- THE CALL TO VIOLENT ACTION -- HE WAS STILL CONVINCED THAT HE WOULD HAVE TO FIND A NEW WAY FORWARD.
"IN TRUTH, HE WAS DESPERATE. HIS ONLY CHOICE WAS TO DIVE DEEP WITHIN HIMSELF... NO MATTER WHAT HE MIGHT FIND THERE.

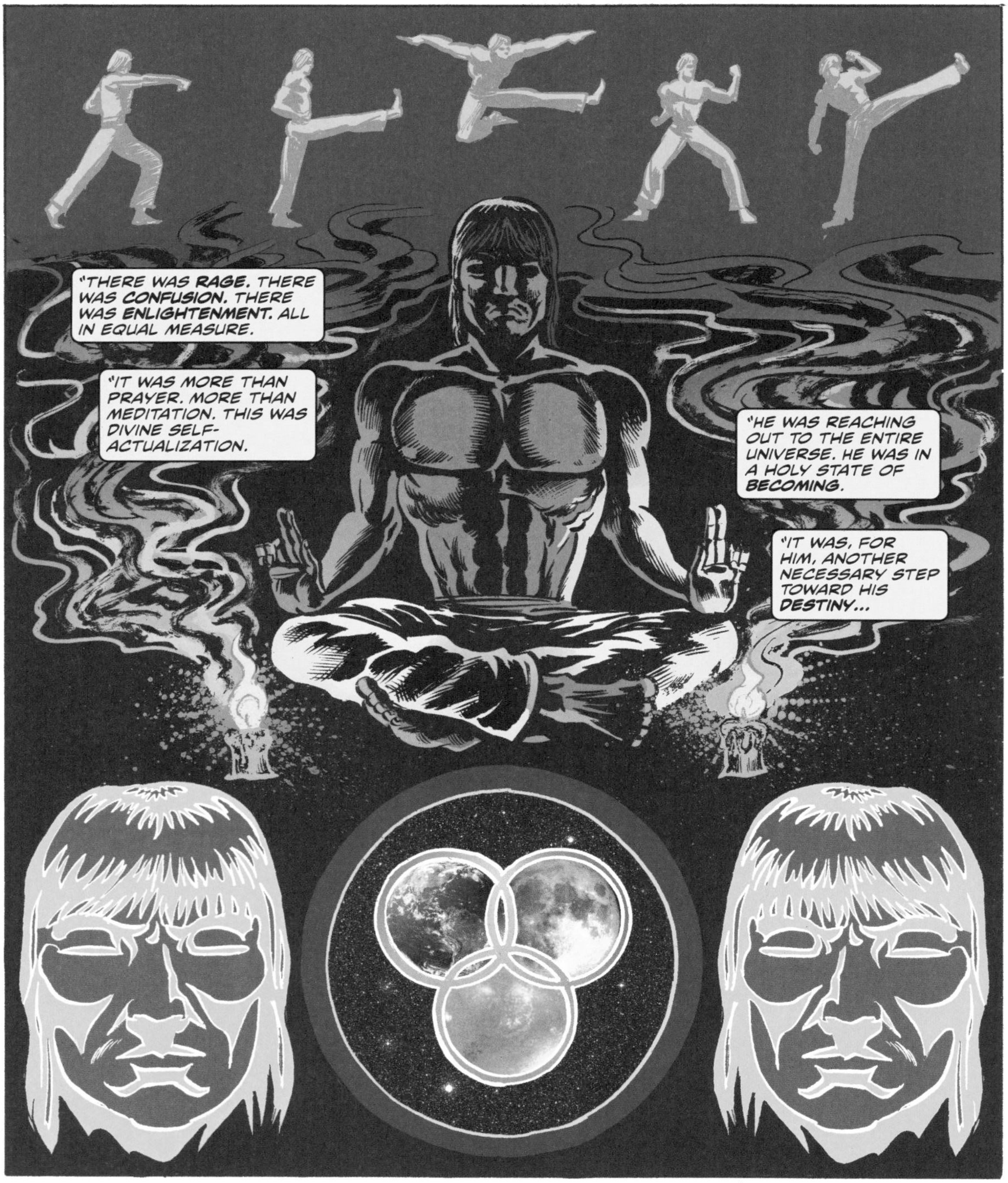
"THERE WAS RAGE. THERE WAS CONFUSION. THERE WAS ENLIGHTENMENT. ALL IN EQUAL MEASURE.
"IT WAS MORE THAN PRAYER. MORE THAN MEDITATION. THIS WAS DIVINE SELF-ACTUALIZATION.
"HE WAS REACHING OUT TO THE ENTIRE UNIVERSE. HE WAS IN A HOLY STATE OF BECOMING.
"IT WAS, FOR HIM, ANOTHER NECESSARY STEP TOWARD HIS DESTINY...

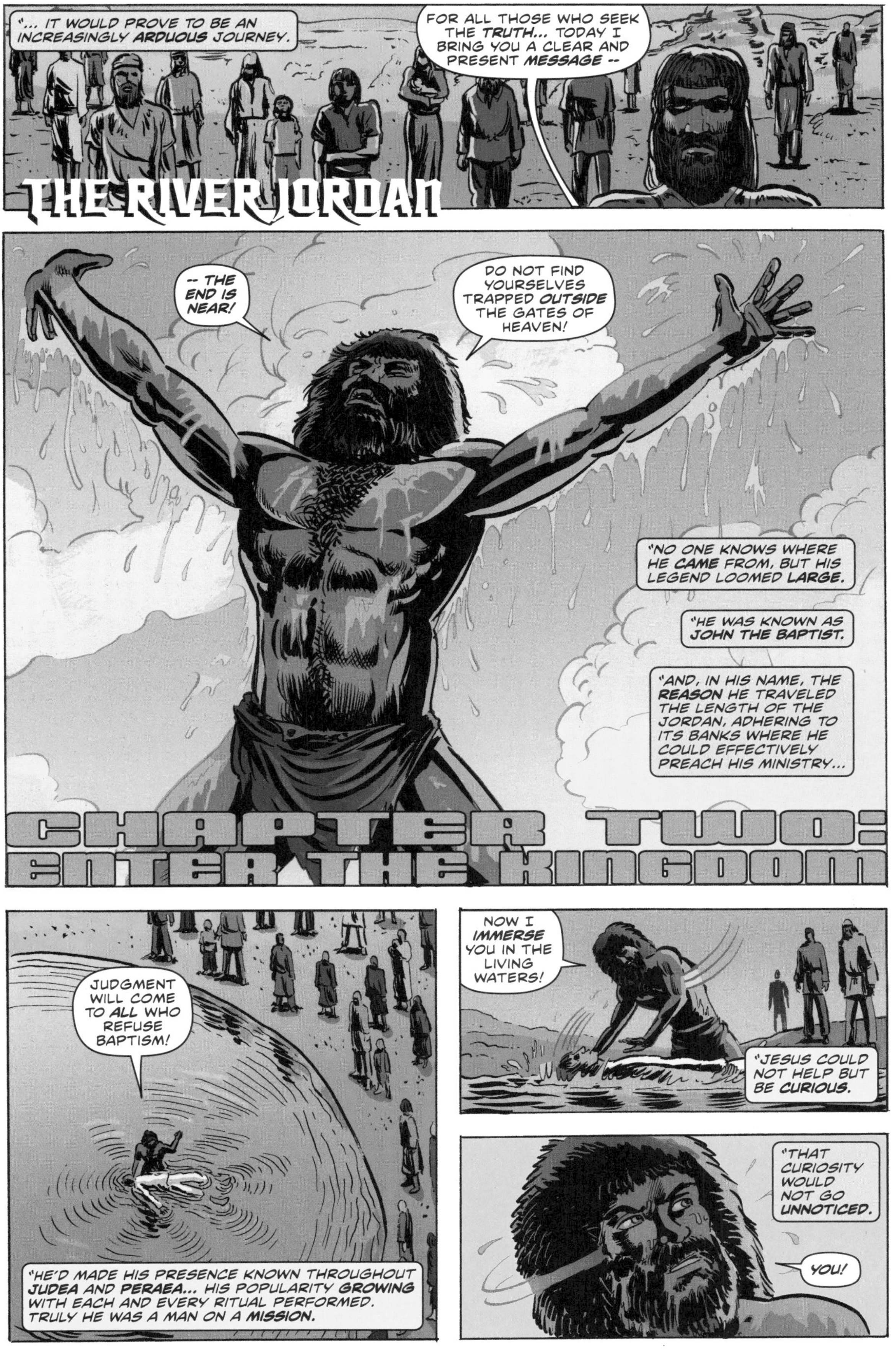
"... IT WOULD PROVE TO BE AN INCREASINGLY ARDUOUS JOURNEY.
FOR ALL THOSE WHO SEEK THE TRUTH... TODAY I BRING YOU A CLEAR AND PRESENT MESSAGE --
THE RIVER JORDAN
-- THE END IS NEAR!
DO NOT FIND YOURSELVES TRAPPED OUTSIDE THE GATES OF HEAVEN!
"NO ONE KNOWS WHERE HE CAME FROM, BUT HIS LEGEND LOOMED LARGE.
"HE WAS KNOWN AS JOHN THE BAPTIST.
"AND, IN HIS NAME, THE REASON HE TRAVELED THE LENGTH OF THE JORDAN, ADHERING TO ITS BANKS WHERE HE COULD EFFECTIVELY PREACH HIS MINISTRY...
CHAPTER TWO: ENTER THE KINGDOM
JUDGMENT WILL COME TO ALL WHO REFUSE BAPTISM!
"HE'D MADE HIS PRESENCE KNOWN THROUGHOUT JUDEA AND PERAEA... HIS POPULARITY GROWING WITH EACH AND EVERY RITUAL PERFORMED. TRULY HE WAS A MAN ON A MISSION.
NOW I IMMERSE YOU IN THE LIVING WATERS!
"JESUS COULD NOT HELP BUT BE CURIOUS.
"THAT CURIOSITY WOULD NOT GO UNNOTICED.
YOU!

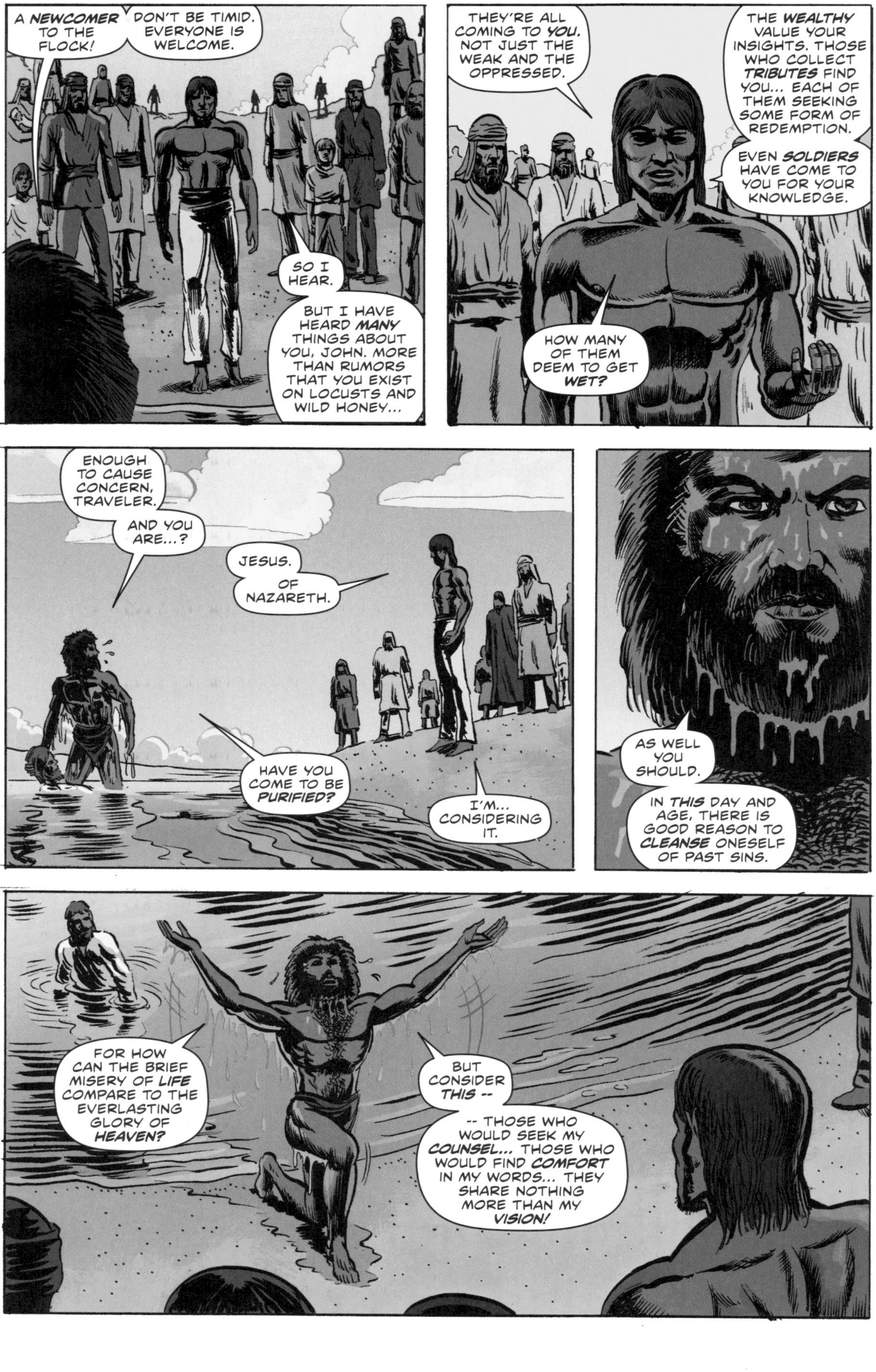
A NEWCOMER TO THE FLOCK!
DON'T BE TIMID. EVERYONE IS WELCOME.
SO I HEAR.
BUT I HAVE HEARD MANY THINGS ABOUT YOU, JOHN. MORE THAN RUMORS THAT YOU EXIST ON LOCUSTS AND WILD HONEY...
THEY'RE ALL COMING TO YOU. NOT JUST THE WEAK AND THE OPPRESSED.
THE WEALTHY VALUE YOUR INSIGHTS. THOSE WHO COLLECT TRIBUTES FIND YOU... EACH OF THEM SEEKING SOME FORM OF REDEMPTION.
EVEN SOLDIERS HAVE COME TO YOU FOR YOUR KNOWLEDGE.
HOW MANY OF THEM DEEM TO GET WET?
ENOUGH TO CAUSE CONCERN, TRAVELER.
AND YOU ARE...?
JESUS.
OF NAZARETH.
HAVE YOU COME TO BE PURIFIED?
I'M... CONSIDERING IT.
AS WELL YOU SHOULD.
IN THIS DAY AND AGE, THERE IS GOOD REASON TO CLEANSE ONESELF OF PAST SINS.
FOR HOW CAN THE BRIEF MISERY OF LIFE COMPARE TO THE EVERLASTING GLORY OF HEAVEN?
BUT CONSIDER THIS --
-- THOSE WHO WOULD SEEK MY COUNSEL... THOSE WHO WOULD FIND COMFORT IN MY WORDS... THEY SHARE NOTHING MORE THAN MY VISION!

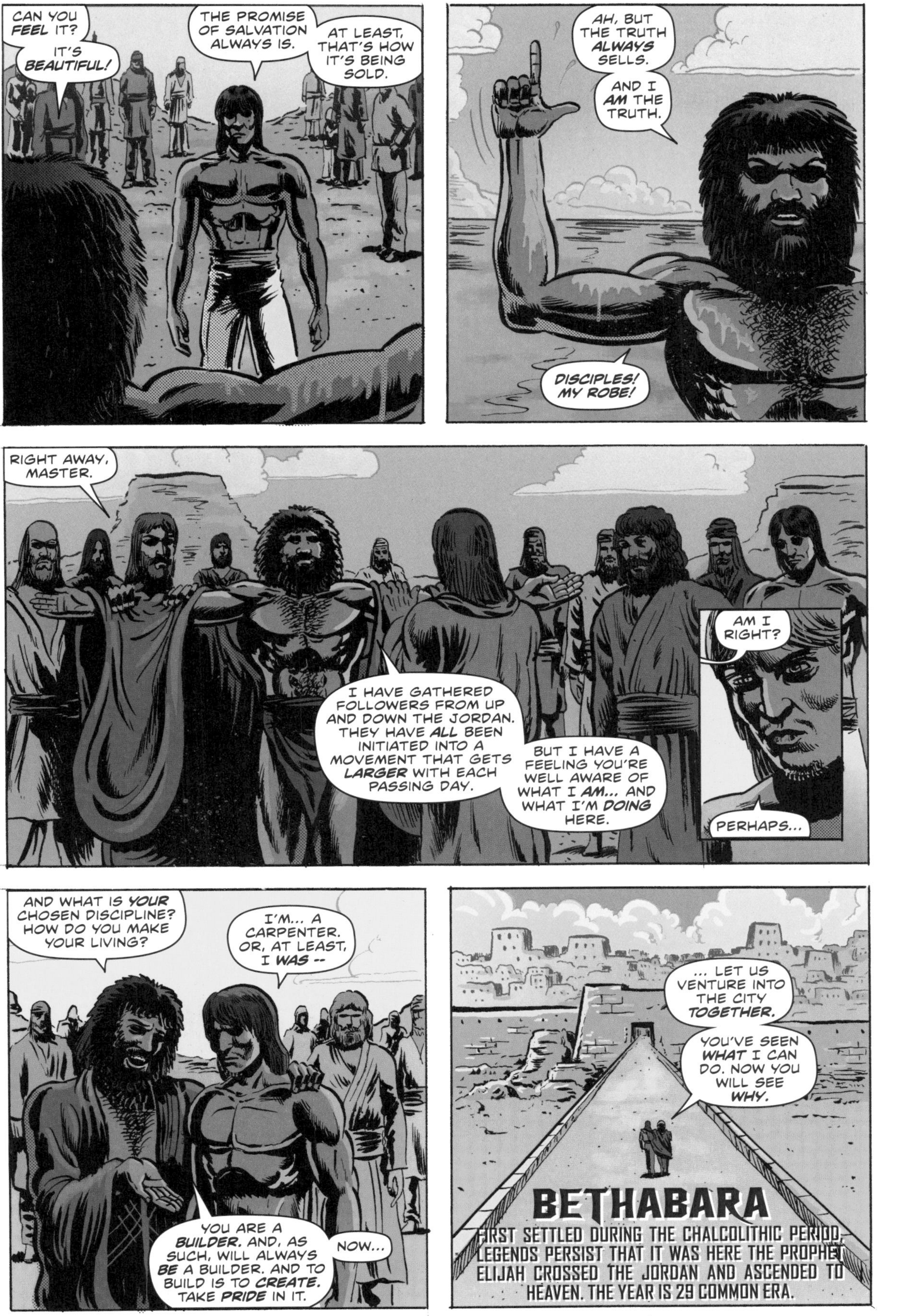
CAN YOU FEEL IT?
IT'S BEAUTIFUL!
THE PROMISE OF SALVATION ALWAYS IS.
AT LEAST, THAT'S HOW IT'S BEING SOLD.
AH, BUT THE TRUTH ALWAYS SELLS.
AND I AM THE TRUTH.
DISCIPLES! MY ROBE!
RIGHT AWAY, MASTER.
I HAVE GATHERED FOLLOWERS FROM UP AND DOWN THE JORDAN. THEY HAVE ALL BEEN INITIATED INTO A MOVEMENT THAT GETS LARGER WITH EACH PASSING DAY.
BUT I HAVE A FEELING YOU'RE WELL AWARE OF WHAT I AM... AND WHAT I'M DOING HERE.
AM I RIGHT?
PERHAPS...
AND WHAT IS YOUR CHOSEN DISCIPLINE? HOW DO YOU MAKE YOUR LIVING?
I'M... A CARPENTER. OR, AT LEAST, I WAS --
YOU ARE A BUILDER. AND, AS SUCH, WILL ALWAYS BE A BUILDER. AND TO BUILD IS TO CREATE. TAKE PRIDE IN IT.
NOW...
... LET US VENTURE INTO THE CITY TOGETHER.
YOU'VE SEEN WHAT I CAN DO. NOW YOU WILL SEE WHY.
BETHABARA
FIRST SETTLED DURING THE CHALCOLITHIC PERIOD, LEGENDS PERSIST THAT IT WAS HERE THE PROPHET ELIJAH CROSSED THE JORDAN AND ASCENDED TO HEAVEN. THE YEAR IS 29 COMMON ERA.

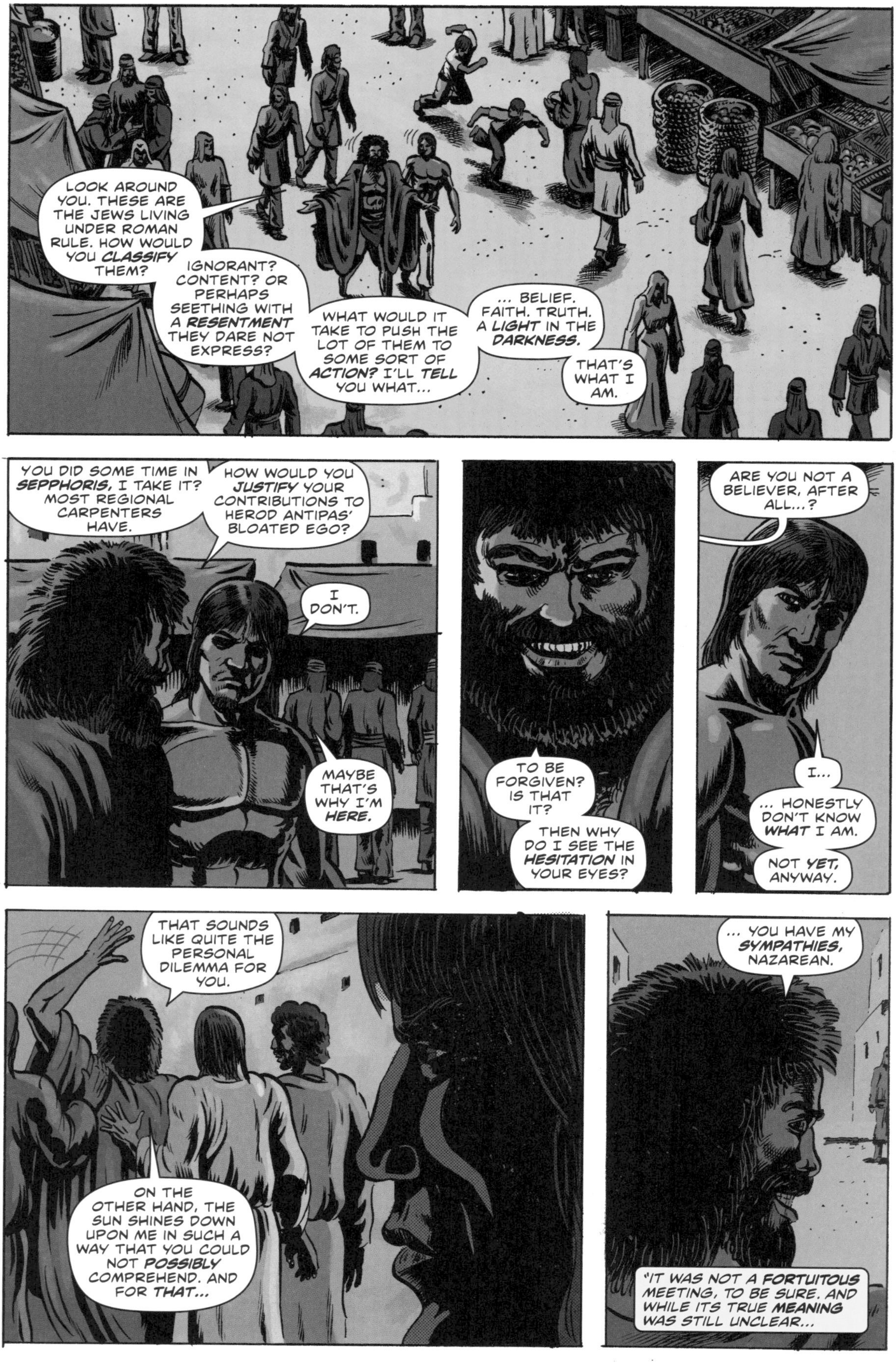
LOOK AROUND YOU. THESE ARE THE JEWS LIVING UNDER ROMAN RULE. HOW WOULD YOU **CLASSIFY** THEM?
IGNORANT? CONTENT? OR PERHAPS SEETHING WITH A **RESENTMENT** THEY DARE NOT EXPRESS?
WHAT WOULD IT TAKE TO PUSH THE LOT OF THEM TO SOME SORT OF **ACTION?** I'LL **TELL** YOU WHAT...
... BELIEF. FAITH. TRUTH. A **LIGHT** IN THE **DARKNESS.**
THAT'S WHAT I AM.
YOU DID SOME TIME IN **SEPPHORIS,** I TAKE IT? MOST REGIONAL CARPENTERS HAVE.
HOW WOULD YOU **JUSTIFY** YOUR CONTRIBUTIONS TO HEROD ANTIPAS' BLOATED EGO?
I DON'T.
MAYBE THAT'S WHY I'M **HERE.**
TO BE FORGIVEN? IS THAT IT?
THEN WHY DO I SEE THE **HESITATION** IN YOUR EYES?
ARE YOU NOT A BELIEVER, AFTER ALL...?
I...
... HONESTLY DON'T KNOW **WHAT** I AM.
NOT **YET,** ANYWAY.
THAT SOUNDS LIKE QUITE THE PERSONAL DILEMMA FOR YOU.
ON THE OTHER HAND, THE SUN SHINES DOWN UPON ME IN SUCH A WAY THAT YOU COULD NOT **POSSIBLY** COMPREHEND. AND FOR **THAT...**
... YOU HAVE MY **SYMPATHIES,** NAZAREAN.
"IT WAS NOT A **FORTUITOUS** MEETING, TO BE SURE. AND WHILE ITS TRUE **MEANING** WAS STILL UNCLEAR...

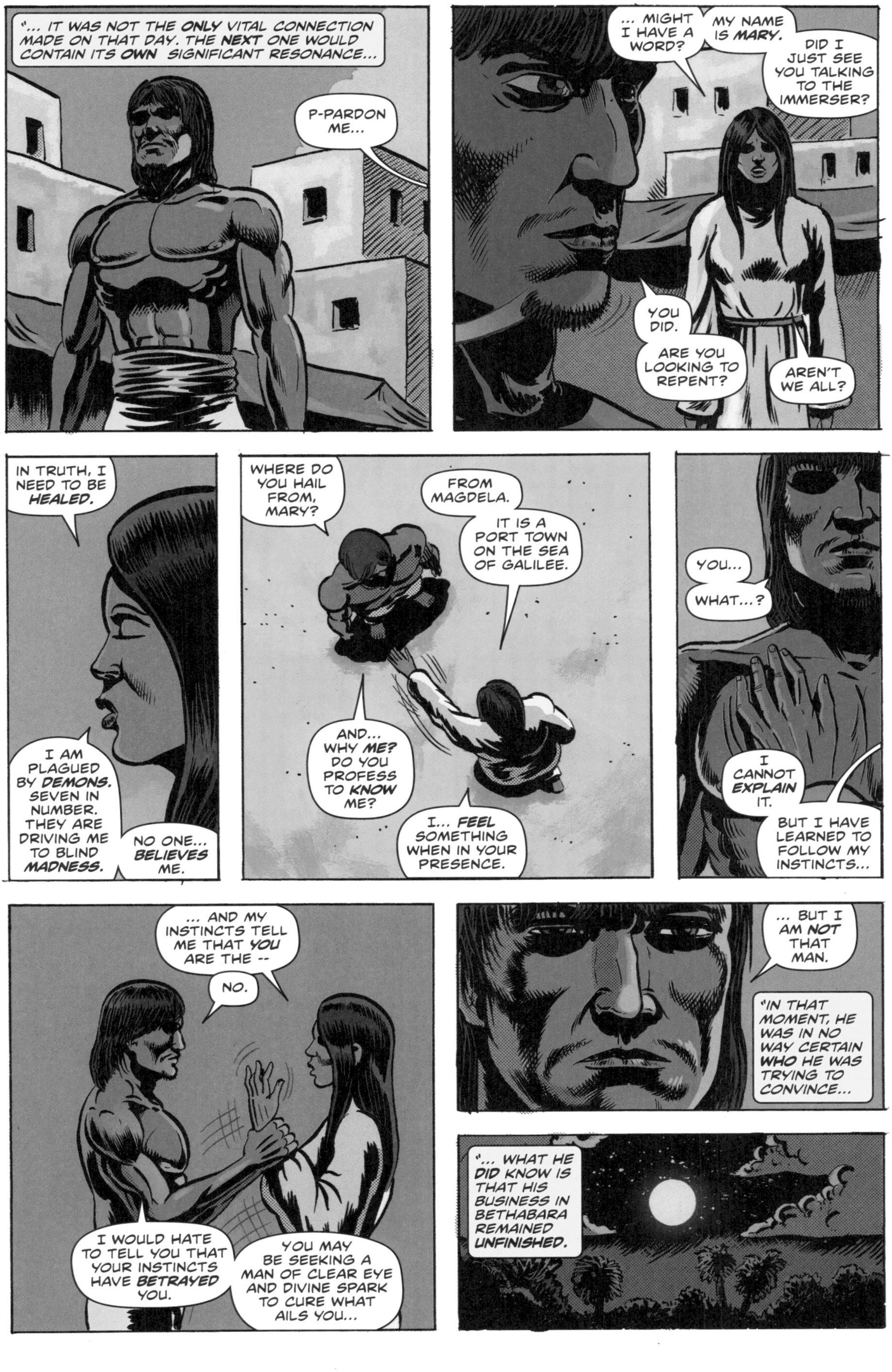

"... IT WAS NOT THE ONLY VITAL CONNECTION MADE ON THAT DAY. THE NEXT ONE WOULD CONTAIN ITS OWN SIGNIFICANT RESONANCE...
P-PARDON ME...
... MIGHT I HAVE A WORD?
MY NAME IS MARY.
DID I JUST SEE YOU TALKING TO THE IMMERSER?
YOU DID.
ARE YOU LOOKING TO REPENT?
AREN'T WE ALL?
IN TRUTH, I NEED TO BE HEALED.
I AM PLAGUED BY DEMONS. SEVEN IN NUMBER. THEY ARE DRIVING ME TO BLIND MADNESS.
NO ONE... BELIEVES ME.
WHERE DO YOU HAIL FROM, MARY?
FROM MAGDELA.
IT IS A PORT TOWN ON THE SEA OF GALILEE.
AND... WHY ME? DO YOU PROFESS TO KNOW ME?
I... FEEL SOMETHING WHEN IN YOUR PRESENCE.
YOU...
WHAT...?
I CANNOT EXPLAIN IT.
BUT I HAVE LEARNED TO FOLLOW MY INSTINCTS...
... AND MY INSTINCTS TELL ME THAT YOU ARE THE --
NO.
I WOULD HATE TO TELL YOU THAT YOUR INSTINCTS HAVE BETRAYED YOU.
YOU MAY BE SEEKING A MAN OF CLEAR EYE AND DIVINE SPARK TO CURE WHAT AILS YOU...
... BUT I AM NOT THAT MAN.
"IN THAT MOMENT, HE WAS IN NO WAY CERTAIN WHO HE WAS TRYING TO CONVINCE...
"... WHAT HE DID KNOW IS THAT HIS BUSINESS IN BETHABARA REMAINED UNFINISHED.

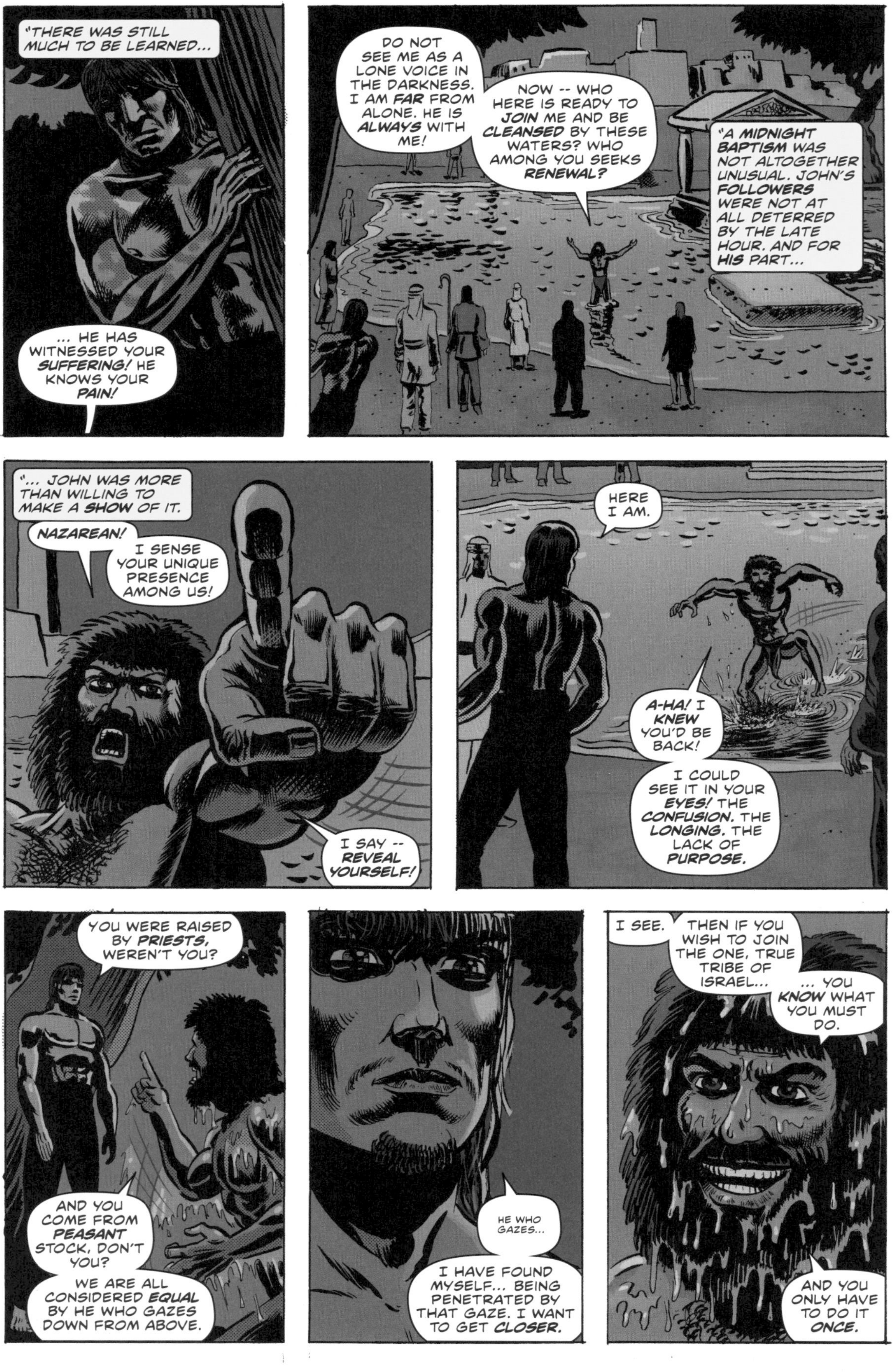
"THERE WAS STILL MUCH TO BE LEARNED...
... HE HAS WITNESSED YOUR SUFFERING! HE KNOWS YOUR PAIN!
DO NOT SEE ME AS A LONE VOICE IN THE DARKNESS. I AM FAR FROM ALONE. HE IS ALWAYS WITH ME!
NOW -- WHO HERE IS READY TO JOIN ME AND BE CLEANSED BY THESE WATERS? WHO AMONG YOU SEEKS RENEWAL?
"A MIDNIGHT BAPTISM WAS NOT ALTOGETHER UNUSUAL. JOHN'S FOLLOWERS WERE NOT AT ALL DETERRED BY THE LATE HOUR. AND FOR HIS PART...
"... JOHN WAS MORE THAN WILLING TO MAKE A SHOW OF IT.
NAZAREAN!
I SENSE YOUR UNIQUE PRESENCE AMONG US!
I SAY -- REVEAL YOURSELF!
HERE I AM.
A-HA! I KNEW YOU'D BE BACK!
I COULD SEE IT IN YOUR EYES! THE CONFUSION. THE LONGING. THE LACK OF PURPOSE.
YOU WERE RAISED BY PRIESTS, WEREN'T YOU?
AND YOU COME FROM PEASANT STOCK, DON'T YOU?
WE ARE ALL CONSIDERED EQUAL BY HE WHO GAZES DOWN FROM ABOVE.
HE WHO GAZES...
I HAVE FOUND MYSELF... BEING PENETRATED BY THAT GAZE. I WANT TO GET CLOSER.
I SEE.
THEN IF YOU WISH TO JOIN THE ONE, TRUE TRIBE OF ISRAEL...
... YOU KNOW WHAT YOU MUST DO.
AND YOU ONLY HAVE TO DO IT ONCE.

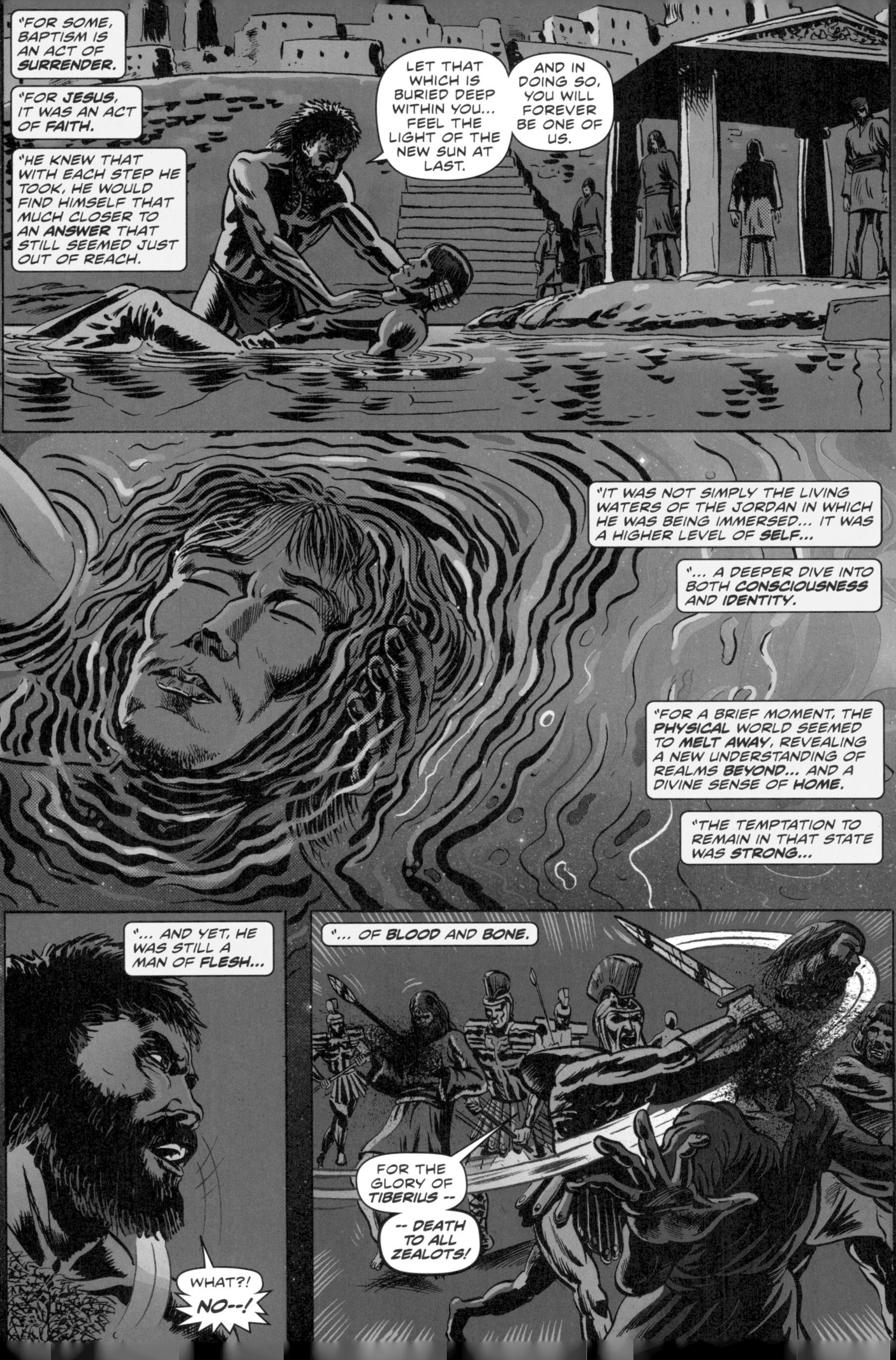
"FOR SOME, BAPTISM IS AN ACT OF SURRENDER.
"FOR JESUS, IT WAS AN ACT OF FAITH.
"HE KNEW THAT WITH EACH STEP HE TOOK, HE WOULD FIND HIMSELF THAT MUCH CLOSER TO AN ANSWER THAT STILL SEEMED JUST OUT OF REACH.
LET THAT WHICH IS BURIED DEEP WITHIN YOU... FEEL THE LIGHT OF THE NEW SUN AT LAST.
AND IN DOING SO, YOU WILL FOREVER BE ONE OF US.
"IT WAS NOT SIMPLY THE LIVING WATERS OF THE JORDAN IN WHICH HE WAS BEING IMMERSED... IT WAS A HIGHER LEVEL OF SELF...
"... A DEEPER DIVE INTO BOTH CONSCIOUSNESS AND IDENTITY.
"FOR A BRIEF MOMENT, THE PHYSICAL WORLD SEEMED TO MELT AWAY, REVEALING A NEW UNDERSTANDING OF REALMS BEYOND... AND A DIVINE SENSE OF HOME.
"THE TEMPTATION TO REMAIN IN THAT STATE WAS STRONG...
"... AND YET, HE WAS STILL A MAN OF FLESH...
WHAT?! NO--!
"... OF BLOOD AND BONE.
FOR THE GLORY OF TIBERIUS --
-- DEATH TO ALL ZEALOTS!

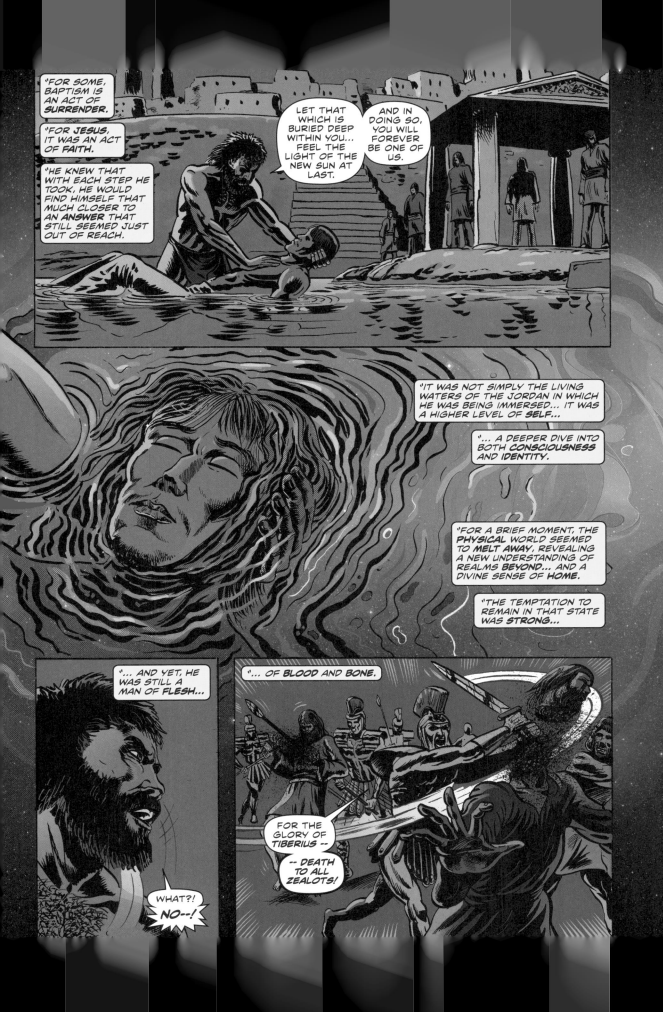

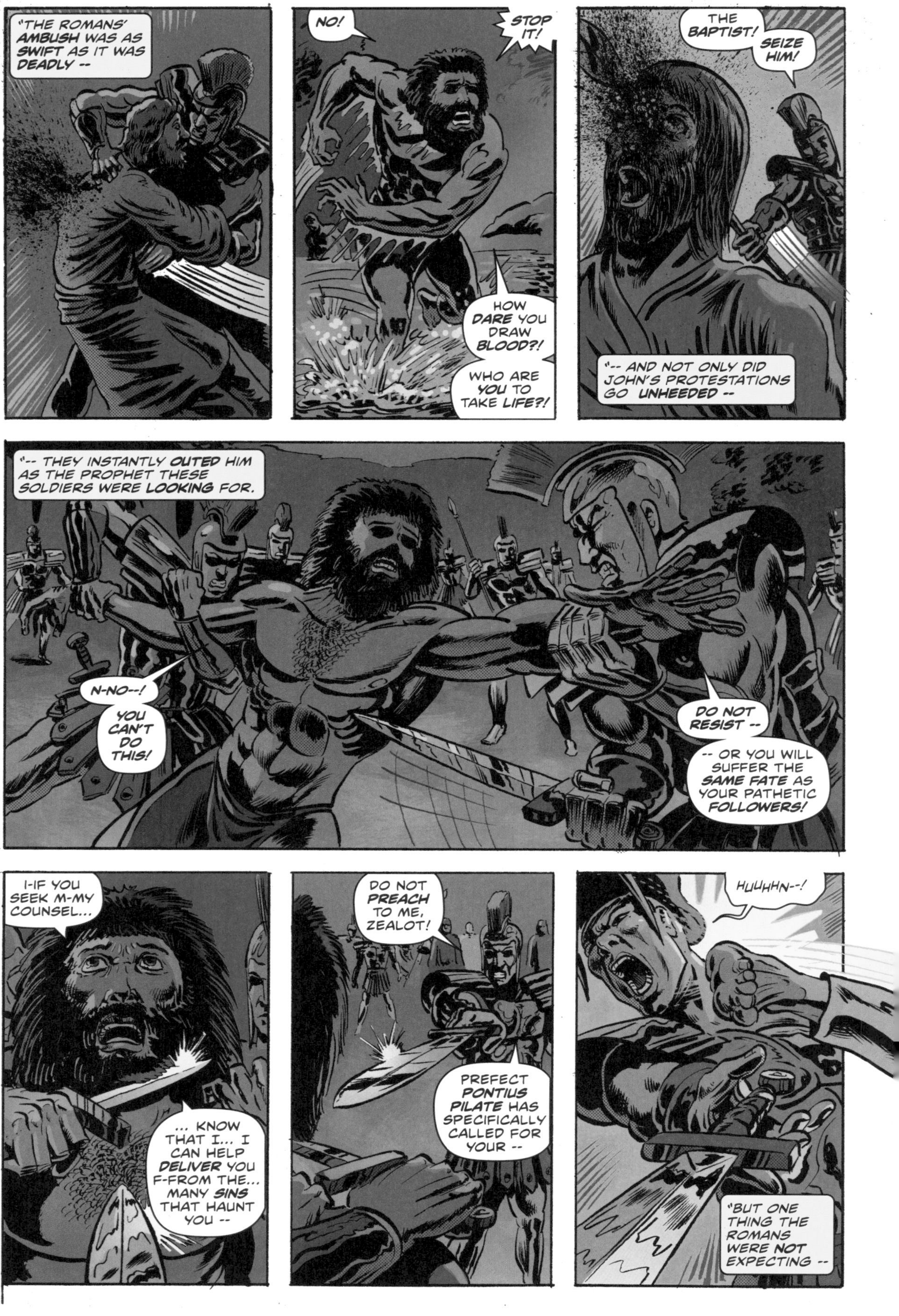
"THE ROMANS' AMBUSH WAS AS SWIFT AS IT WAS DEADLY --
NO!
STOP IT!
HOW DARE YOU DRAW BLOOD?!
WHO ARE YOU TO TAKE LIFE?!
THE BAPTIST!
SEIZE HIM!
"-- AND NOT ONLY DID JOHN'S PROTESTATIONS GO UNHEEDED --
"-- THEY INSTANTLY OUTED HIM AS THE PROPHET THESE SOLDIERS WERE LOOKING FOR.
N-NO--!
YOU CAN'T DO THIS!
DO NOT RESIST --
-- OR YOU WILL SUFFER THE SAME FATE AS YOUR PATHETIC FOLLOWERS!
I-IF YOU SEEK M-MY COUNSEL...
... KNOW THAT I... I CAN HELP DELIVER YOU F-FROM THE... MANY SINS THAT HAUNT YOU --
DO NOT PREACH TO ME, ZEALOT!
PREFECT PONTIUS PILATE HAS SPECIFICALLY CALLED FOR YOUR --
HUUHHN--!
"BUT ONE THING THE ROMANS WERE NOT EXPECTING --

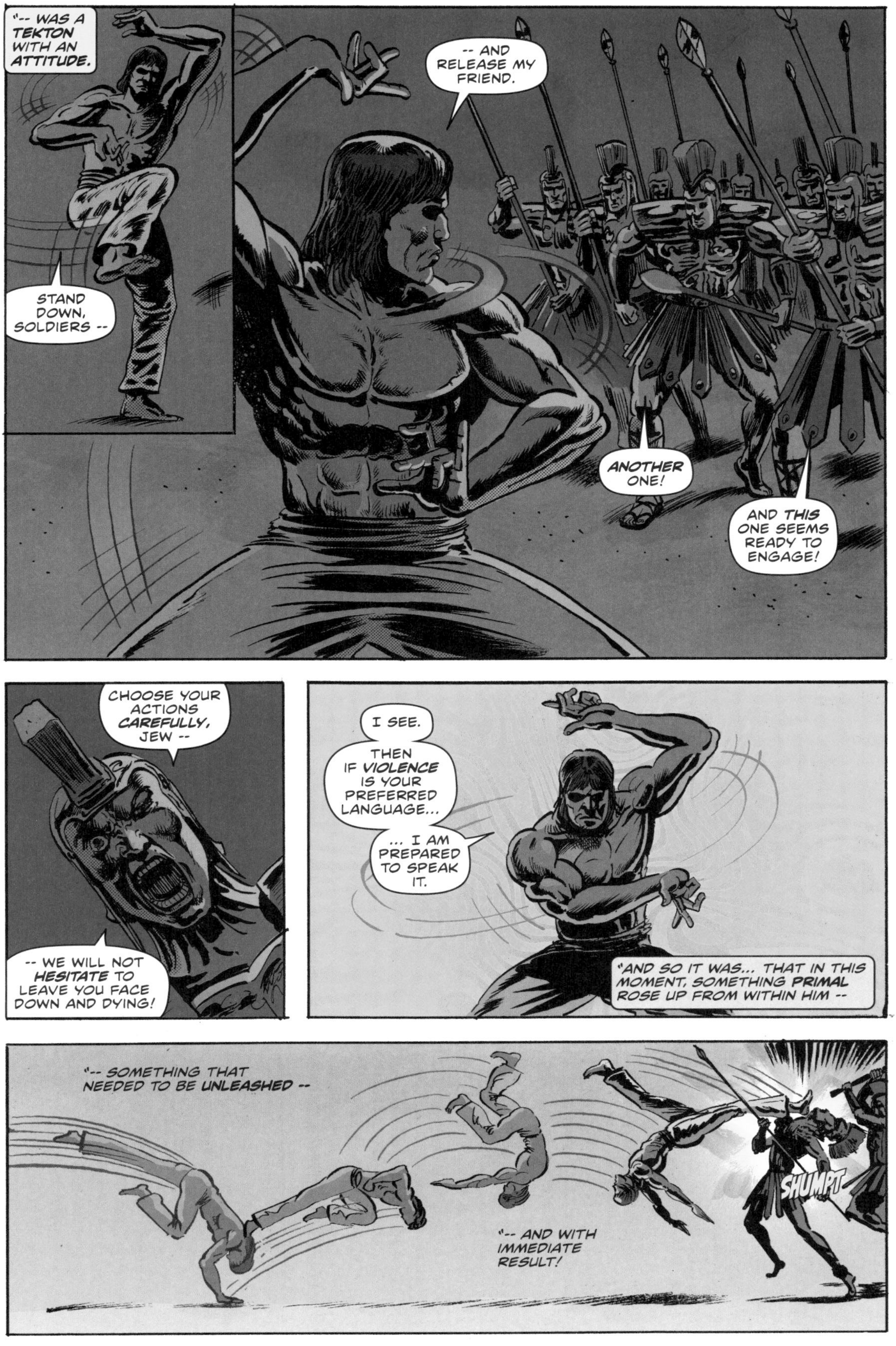
"-- WAS A TEKTON WITH AN ATTITUDE.
STAND DOWN, SOLDIERS --
-- AND RELEASE MY FRIEND.
ANOTHER ONE!
AND THIS ONE SEEMS READY TO ENGAGE!
CHOOSE YOUR ACTIONS CAREFULLY, JEW --
-- WE WILL NOT HESITATE TO LEAVE YOU FACE DOWN AND DYING!
I SEE.
THEN IF VIOLENCE IS YOUR PREFERRED LANGUAGE...
... I AM PREPARED TO SPEAK IT.
"AND SO IT WAS... THAT IN THIS MOMENT, SOMETHING PRIMAL ROSE UP FROM WITHIN HIM --
"-- SOMETHING THAT NEEDED TO BE UNLEASHED --
SHUMPT
"-- AND WITH IMMEDIATE RESULT!

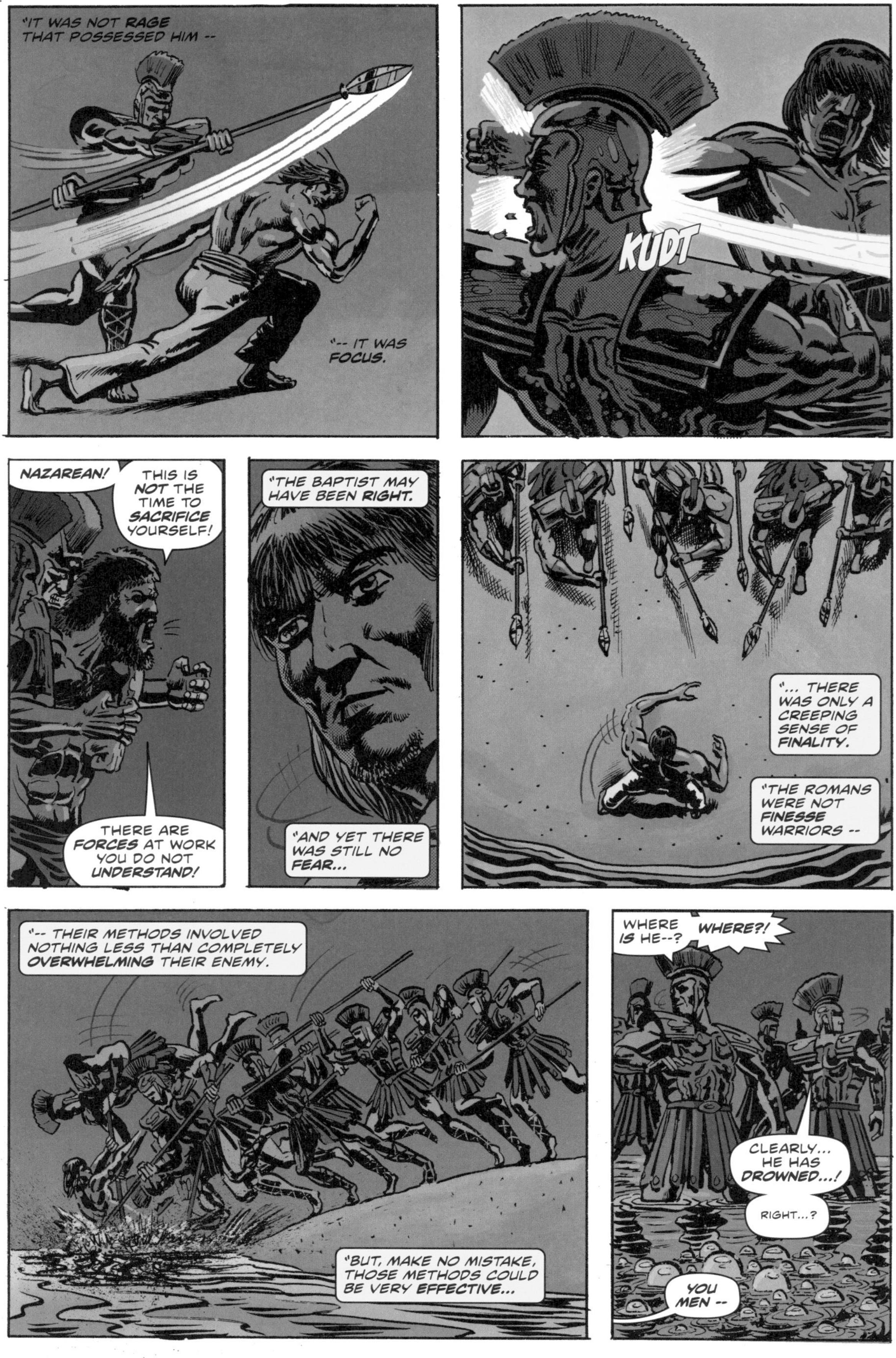
"IT WAS NOT RAGE THAT POSSESSED HIM --
"-- IT WAS FOCUS.
KUDT
NAZAREAN!
THIS IS NOT THE TIME TO SACRIFICE YOURSELF!
THERE ARE FORCES AT WORK YOU DO NOT UNDERSTAND!
"THE BAPTIST MAY HAVE BEEN RIGHT.
"AND YET THERE WAS STILL NO FEAR...
"... THERE WAS ONLY A CREEPING SENSE OF FINALITY.
"THE ROMANS WERE NOT FINESSE WARRIORS --
"-- THEIR METHODS INVOLVED NOTHING LESS THAN COMPLETELY OVERWHELMING THEIR ENEMY.
"BUT, MAKE NO MISTAKE, THOSE METHODS COULD BE VERY EFFECTIVE...
WHERE IS HE--?
WHERE?!
CLEARLY... HE HAS DROWNED...!
RIGHT...?
YOU MEN --

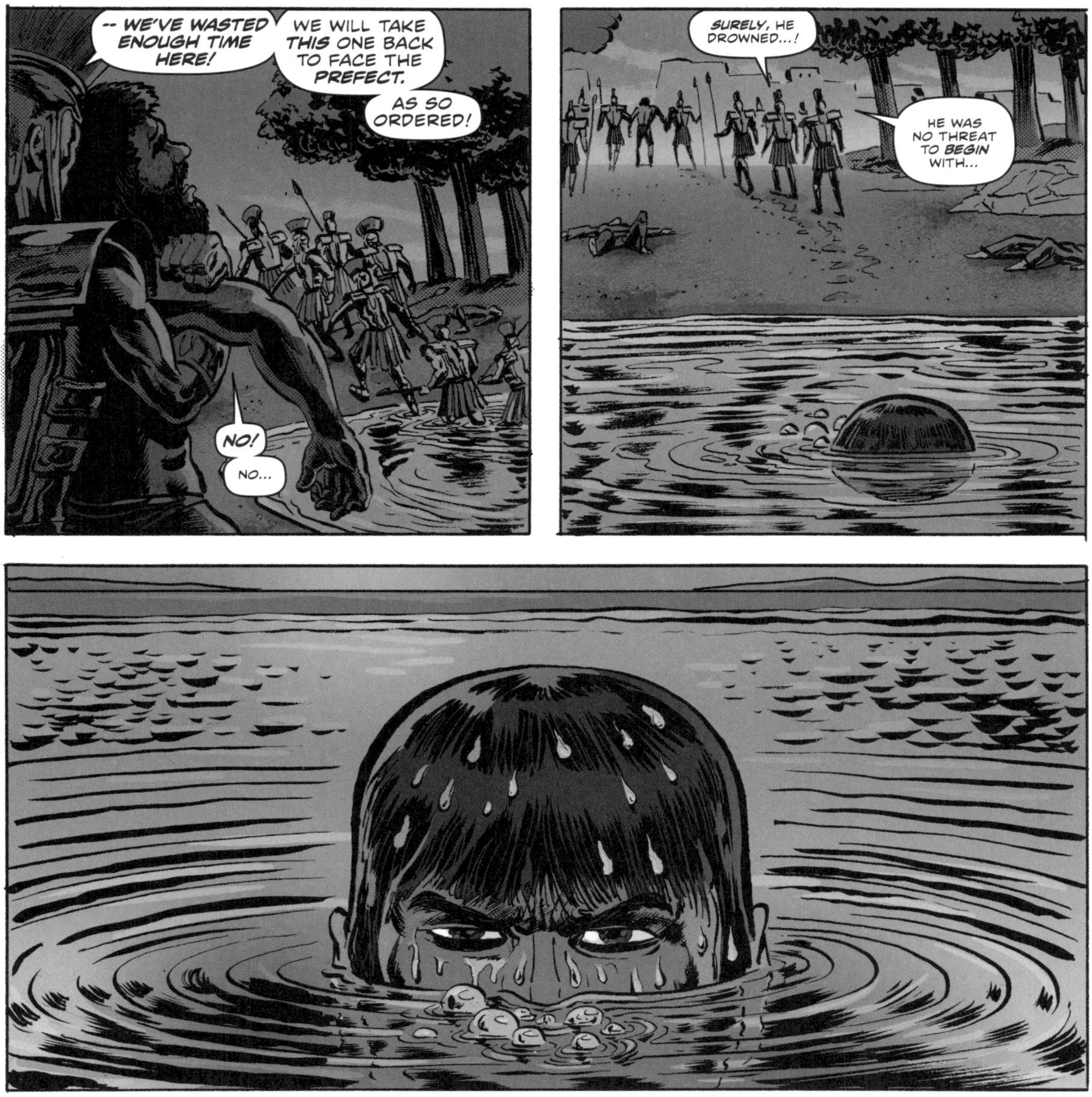
-- WE'VE WASTED ENOUGH TIME HERE!
WE WILL TAKE THIS ONE BACK TO FACE THE PREFECT.
AS SO ORDERED!
NO!
NO...
SURELY, HE DROWNED...!
HE WAS NO THREAT TO BEGIN WITH...

"AND SO IT WAS

THAT HE HAD COMMITTED HIS FIRST TRUE ACT OF OPEN **DEFIANCE.** A BLATANT ACT OF POLITICAL **INSURRECTION** THAT COULD, IN NO WAY, BE DENIED. BUT AT WHAT **COST?**

"NEVERTHELESS, THIS WAS THE MOMENT WHERE HE FINALLY CROSSED OVER AND FULLY **EMBRACED** HIS OWN ZEALOUS NATURE. THE **EVOLUTION** TOWARD **REVOLUTION** HAD BEGUN. NOW HE KNEW FOR CERTAIN THE BLOODY ROAD THAT LAY AHEAD OF HIM. WHETHER OR NOT HE WOULD TRAVEL IT **ALONE** HAD YET TO BE DECIDED. SOON, IT WOULD BE DECIDED **FOR** HIM.

"OF COURSE, THERE WOULD BE DIRE **CONSEQUENCES.** AND NOT JUST FOR JESUS OF NAZARETH...

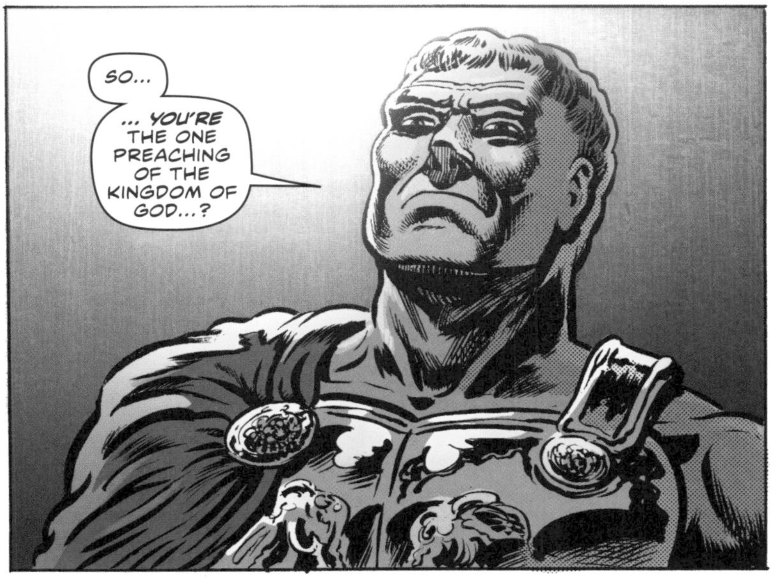
SO...
... YOU'RE THE ONE PREACHING OF THE KINGDOM OF GOD...?

CHAPTER THREE: HOT HANDS OF HEAVEN

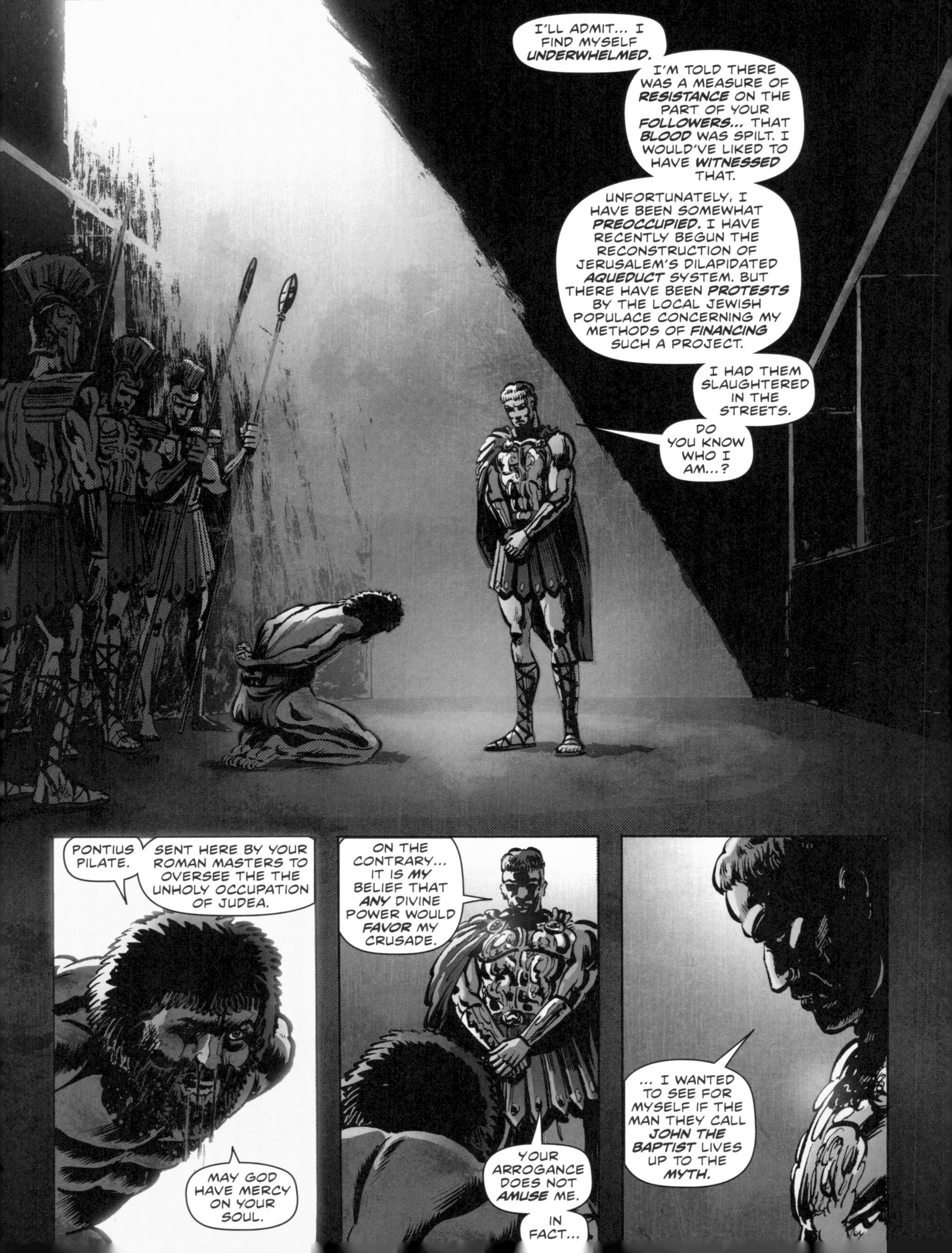
I'LL ADMIT... I FIND MYSELF UNDERWHELMED.
I'M TOLD THERE WAS A MEASURE OF RESISTANCE ON THE PART OF YOUR FOLLOWERS... THAT BLOOD WAS SPILT. I WOULD'VE LIKED TO HAVE WITNESSED THAT.
UNFORTUNATELY, I HAVE BEEN SOMEWHAT PREOCCUPIED. I HAVE RECENTLY BEGUN THE RECONSTRUCTION OF JERUSALEM'S DILAPIDATED AQUEDUCT SYSTEM. BUT THERE HAVE BEEN PROTESTS BY THE LOCAL JEWISH POPULACE CONCERNING MY METHODS OF FINANCING SUCH A PROJECT.
I HAD THEM SLAUGHTERED IN THE STREETS.
DO YOU KNOW WHO I AM...?
PONTIUS PILATE.
SENT HERE BY YOUR ROMAN MASTERS TO OVERSEE THE THE UNHOLY OCCUPATION OF JUDEA.
MAY GOD HAVE MERCY ON YOUR SOUL.
ON THE CONTRARY... IT IS MY BELIEF THAT ANY DIVINE POWER WOULD FAVOR MY CRUSADE.
YOUR ARROGANCE DOES NOT AMUSE ME.
IN FACT...
... I WANTED TO SEE FOR MYSELF IF THE MAN THEY CALL JOHN THE BAPTIST LIVES UP TO THE MYTH.

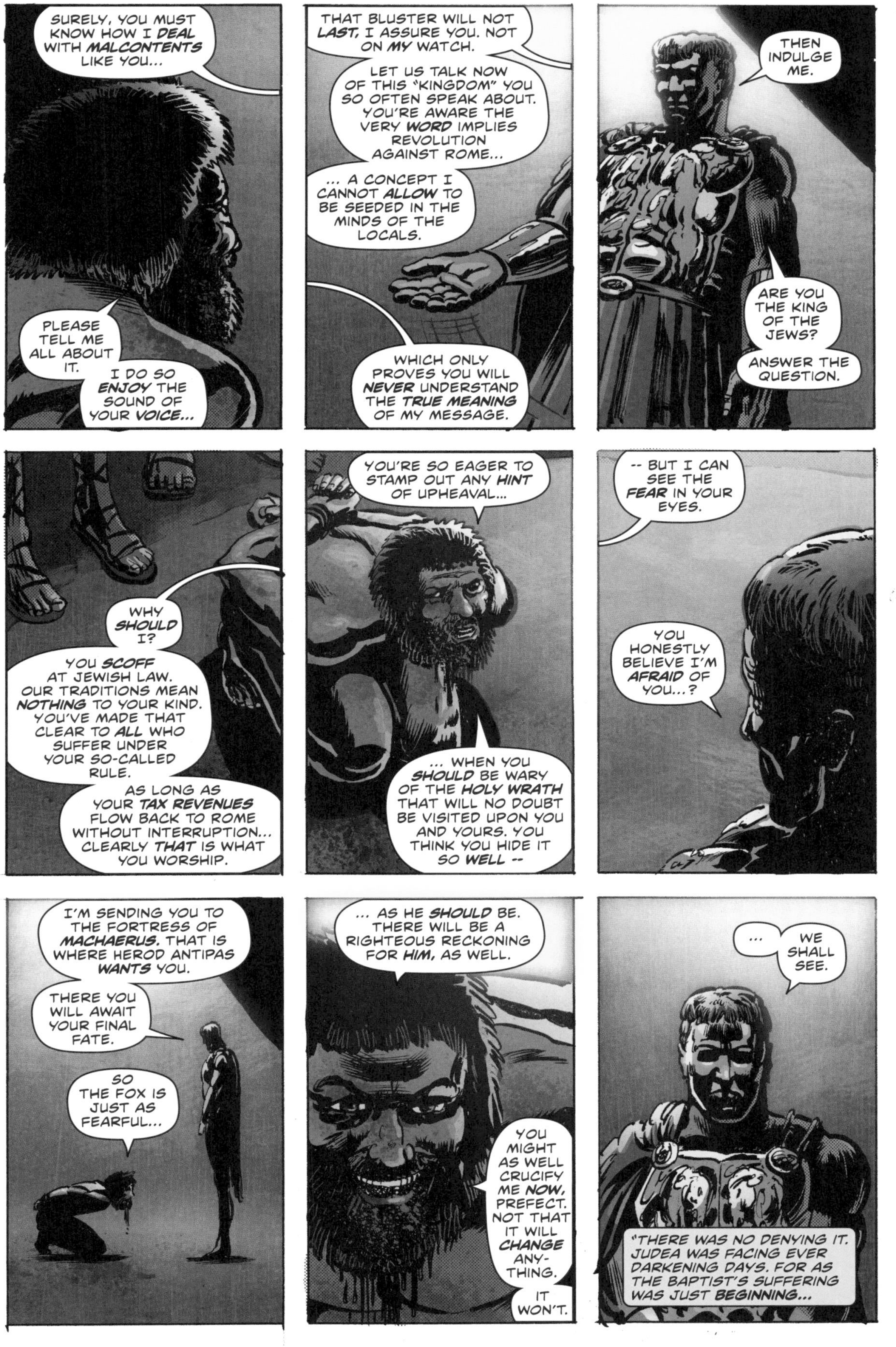
SURELY, YOU MUST KNOW HOW I DEAL WITH MALCONTENTS LIKE YOU...
PLEASE TELL ME ALL ABOUT IT.
I DO SO ENJOY THE SOUND OF YOUR VOICE...
THAT BLUSTER WILL NOT LAST, I ASSURE YOU. NOT ON MY WATCH.
LET US TALK NOW OF THIS "KINGDOM" YOU SO OFTEN SPEAK ABOUT. YOU'RE AWARE THE VERY WORD IMPLIES REVOLUTION AGAINST ROME...
... A CONCEPT I CANNOT ALLOW TO BE SEEDED IN THE MINDS OF THE LOCALS.
WHICH ONLY PROVES YOU WILL NEVER UNDERSTAND THE TRUE MEANING OF MY MESSAGE.
THEN INDULGE ME.
ARE YOU THE KING OF THE JEWS?
ANSWER THE QUESTION.
WHY SHOULD I?
YOU SCOFF AT JEWISH LAW. OUR TRADITIONS MEAN NOTHING TO YOUR KIND. YOU'VE MADE THAT CLEAR TO ALL WHO SUFFER UNDER YOUR SO-CALLED RULE.
AS LONG AS YOUR TAX REVENUES FLOW BACK TO ROME WITHOUT INTERRUPTION... CLEARLY THAT IS WHAT YOU WORSHIP.
YOU'RE SO EAGER TO STAMP OUT ANY HINT OF UPHEAVAL...
... WHEN YOU SHOULD BE WARY OF THE HOLY WRATH THAT WILL NO DOUBT BE VISITED UPON YOU AND YOURS. YOU THINK YOU HIDE IT SO WELL --
-- BUT I CAN SEE THE FEAR IN YOUR EYES.
YOU HONESTLY BELIEVE I'M AFRAID OF YOU...?
I'M SENDING YOU TO THE FORTRESS OF MACHAERUS. THAT IS WHERE HEROD ANTIPAS WANTS YOU.
THERE YOU WILL AWAIT YOUR FINAL FATE.
SO THE FOX IS JUST AS FEARFUL...
... AS HE SHOULD BE. THERE WILL BE A RIGHTEOUS RECKONING FOR HIM, AS WELL.
YOU MIGHT AS WELL CRUCIFY ME NOW, PREFECT. NOT THAT IT WILL CHANGE ANY-THING.
IT WON'T.
...
WE SHALL SEE.
"THERE WAS NO DENYING IT. JUDEA WAS FACING EVER DARKENING DAYS. FOR AS THE BAPTIST'S SUFFERING WAS JUST BEGINNING...

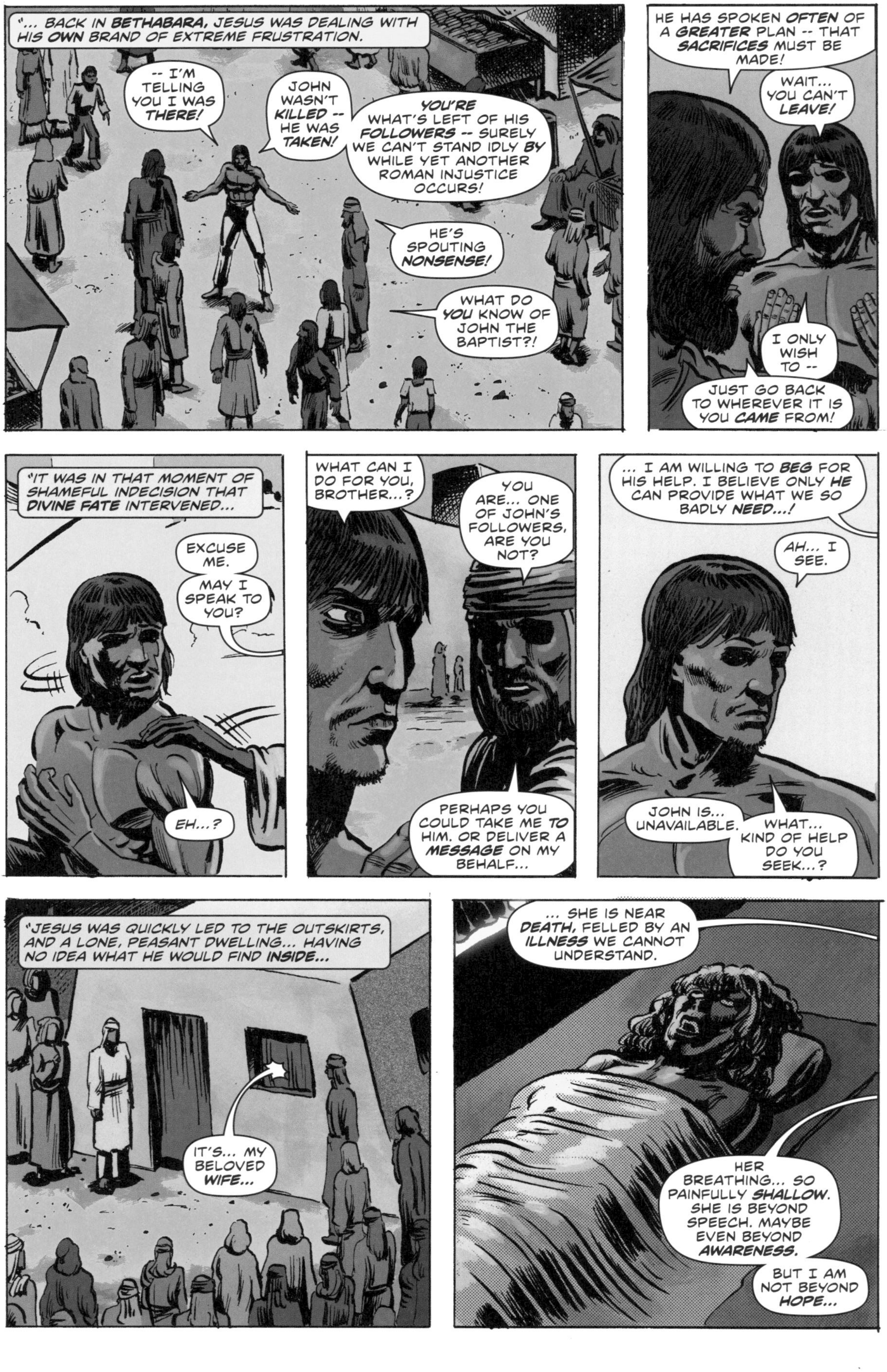
"... BACK IN BETHABARA, JESUS WAS DEALING WITH HIS OWN BRAND OF EXTREME FRUSTRATION.
-- I'M TELLING YOU I WAS THERE!
JOHN WASN'T KILLED -- HE WAS TAKEN!
YOU'RE WHAT'S LEFT OF HIS FOLLOWERS -- SURELY WE CAN'T STAND IDLY BY WHILE YET ANOTHER ROMAN INJUSTICE OCCURS!
HE'S SPOUTING NONSENSE!
WHAT DO YOU KNOW OF JOHN THE BAPTIST?!
HE HAS SPOKEN OFTEN OF A GREATER PLAN -- THAT SACRIFICES MUST BE MADE!
WAIT... YOU CAN'T LEAVE!
I ONLY WISH TO --
JUST GO BACK TO WHEREVER IT IS YOU CAME FROM!
"IT WAS IN THAT MOMENT OF SHAMEFUL INDECISION THAT DIVINE FATE INTERVENED...
EXCUSE ME.
MAY I SPEAK TO YOU?
EH...?
WHAT CAN I DO FOR YOU, BROTHER...?
YOU ARE... ONE OF JOHN'S FOLLOWERS, ARE YOU NOT?
PERHAPS YOU COULD TAKE ME TO HIM. OR DELIVER A MESSAGE ON MY BEHALF...
... I AM WILLING TO BEG FOR HIS HELP. I BELIEVE ONLY HE CAN PROVIDE WHAT WE SO BADLY NEED...!
AH... I SEE.
JOHN IS... UNAVAILABLE.
WHAT... KIND OF HELP DO YOU SEEK...?
"JESUS WAS QUICKLY LED TO THE OUTSKIRTS, AND A LONE, PEASANT DWELLING... HAVING NO IDEA WHAT HE WOULD FIND INSIDE...
IT'S... MY BELOVED WIFE...
... SHE IS NEAR DEATH, FELLED BY AN ILLNESS WE CANNOT UNDERSTAND.
HER BREATHING... SO PAINFULLY SHALLOW. SHE IS BEYOND SPEECH. MAYBE EVEN BEYOND AWARENESS.
BUT I AM NOT BEYOND HOPE...

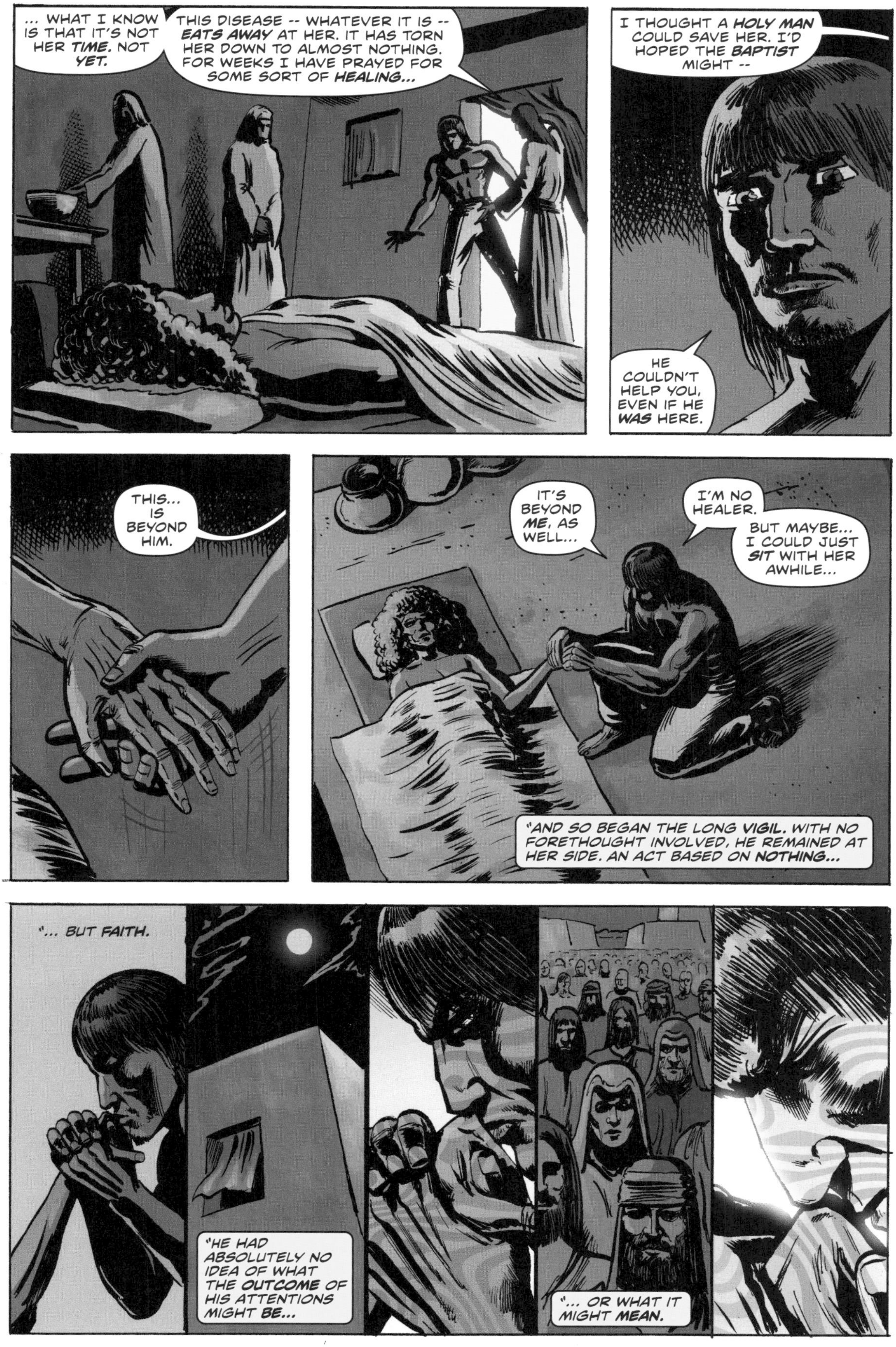
... WHAT I KNOW IS THAT IT'S NOT HER *TIME.* NOT *YET.*
THIS DISEASE -- WHATEVER IT IS -- *EATS AWAY* AT HER. IT HAS TORN HER DOWN TO ALMOST NOTHING. FOR WEEKS I HAVE PRAYED FOR SOME SORT OF *HEALING...*
I THOUGHT A *HOLY MAN* COULD SAVE HER. I'D HOPED THE *BAPTIST* MIGHT --
HE COULDN'T HELP YOU, EVEN IF HE *WAS* HERE.
THIS... IS BEYOND HIM.
IT'S BEYOND *ME,* AS WELL...
I'M NO HEALER.
BUT MAYBE... I COULD JUST *SIT* WITH HER AWHILE...
"AND SO BEGAN THE LONG *VIGIL.* WITH NO FORETHOUGHT INVOLVED, HE REMAINED AT HER SIDE. AN ACT BASED ON *NOTHING...*
"... BUT *FAITH.*
"HE HAD ABSOLUTELY NO IDEA OF WHAT THE *OUTCOME* OF HIS ATTENTIONS MIGHT *BE...*
"... OR WHAT IT MIGHT *MEAN.*

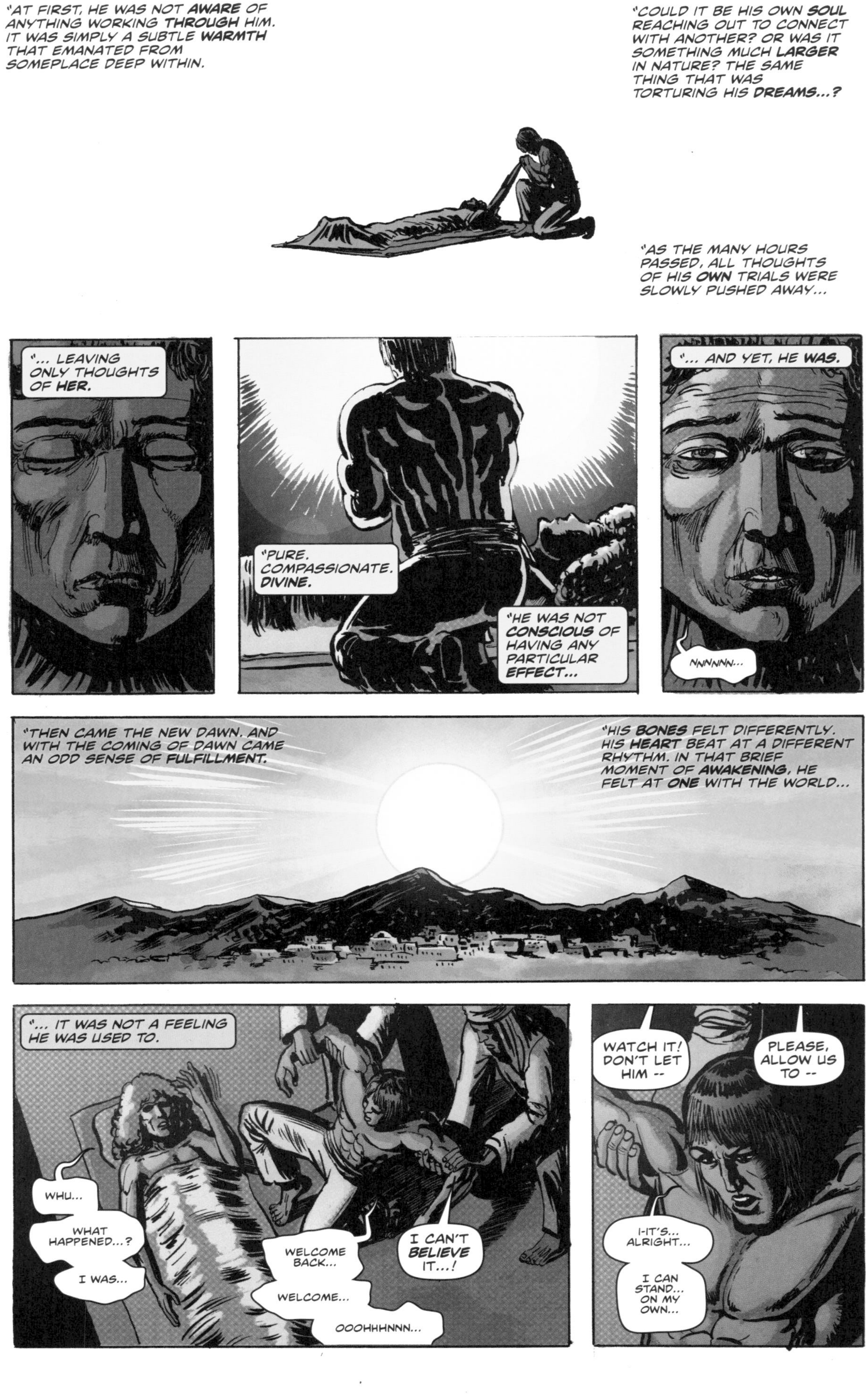
"AT FIRST, HE WAS NOT AWARE OF ANYTHING WORKING THROUGH HIM. IT WAS SIMPLY A SUBTLE WARMTH THAT EMANATED FROM SOMEPLACE DEEP WITHIN.
"COULD IT BE HIS OWN SOUL REACHING OUT TO CONNECT WITH ANOTHER? OR WAS IT SOMETHING MUCH LARGER IN NATURE? THE SAME THING THAT WAS TORTURING HIS DREAMS...?
"AS THE MANY HOURS PASSED, ALL THOUGHTS OF HIS OWN TRIALS WERE SLOWLY PUSHED AWAY...
"... LEAVING ONLY THOUGHTS OF HER.
"PURE. COMPASSIONATE. DIVINE.
"HE WAS NOT CONSCIOUS OF HAVING ANY PARTICULAR EFFECT...
"... AND YET, HE WAS.
NNNNNN...
"THEN CAME THE NEW DAWN. AND WITH THE COMING OF DAWN CAME AN ODD SENSE OF FULFILLMENT.
"HIS BONES FELT DIFFERENTLY. HIS HEART BEAT AT A DIFFERENT RHYTHM. IN THAT BRIEF MOMENT OF AWAKENING, HE FELT AT ONE WITH THE WORLD...
"... IT WAS NOT A FEELING HE WAS USED TO.
WHU...
WHAT HAPPENED...?
I WAS...
WELCOME BACK...
WELCOME...
OOOHHHNNN...
I CAN'T BELIEVE IT...!
WATCH IT! DON'T LET HIM --
PLEASE, ALLOW US TO --
I-IT'S... ALRIGHT...
I CAN STAND... ON MY OWN...

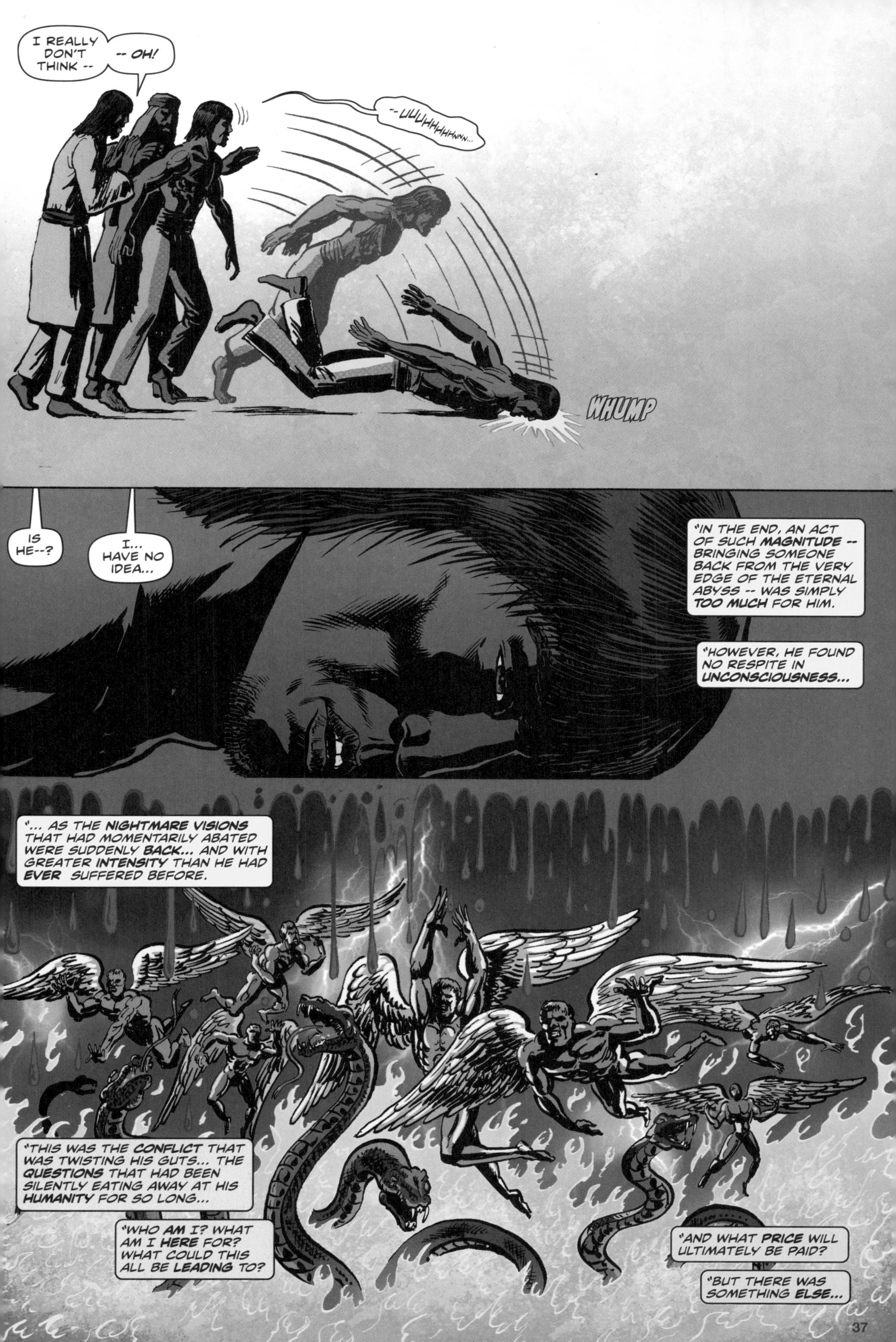
I REALLY DON'T THINK --
-- OH!
--UUUHHHHHNN...
WHUMP
IS HE--?
I... HAVE NO IDEA...
"IN THE END, AN ACT OF SUCH MAGNITUDE -- BRINGING SOMEONE BACK FROM THE VERY EDGE OF THE ETERNAL ABYSS -- WAS SIMPLY TOO MUCH FOR HIM.
"HOWEVER, HE FOUND NO RESPITE IN UNCONSCIOUSNESS...
"... AS THE NIGHTMARE VISIONS THAT HAD MOMENTARILY ABATED WERE SUDDENLY BACK... AND WITH GREATER INTENSITY THAN HE HAD EVER SUFFERED BEFORE.
"THIS WAS THE CONFLICT THAT WAS TWISTING HIS GUTS... THE QUESTIONS THAT HAD BEEN SILENTLY EATING AWAY AT HIS HUMANITY FOR SO LONG...
"WHO AM I? WHAT AM I HERE FOR? WHAT COULD THIS ALL BE LEADING TO?
"AND WHAT PRICE WILL ULTIMATELY BE PAID?
"BUT THERE WAS SOMETHING ELSE...

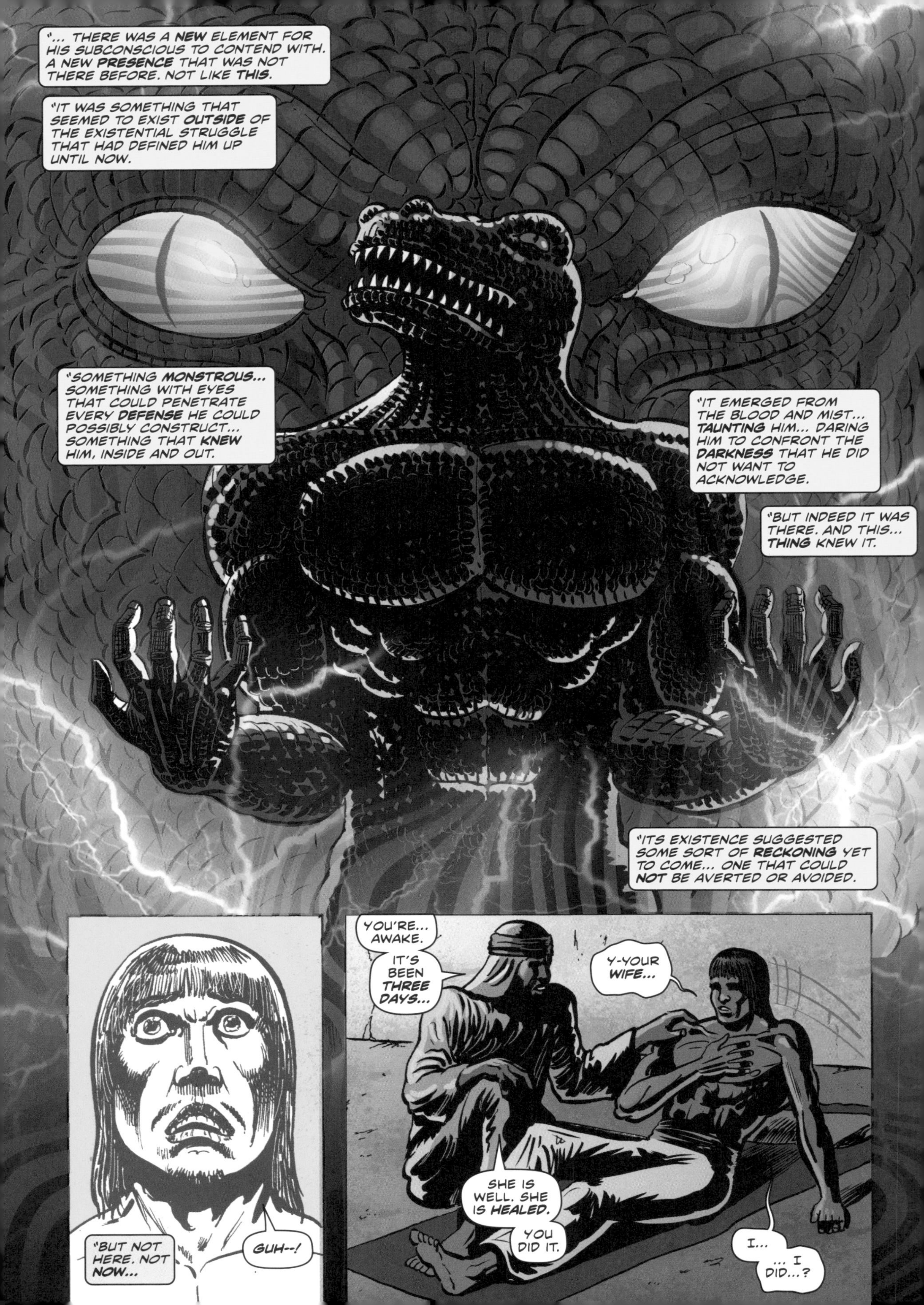
"... THERE WAS A NEW ELEMENT FOR HIS SUBCONSCIOUS TO CONTEND WITH. A NEW PRESENCE THAT WAS NOT THERE BEFORE. NOT LIKE THIS.
"IT WAS SOMETHING THAT SEEMED TO EXIST OUTSIDE OF THE EXISTENTIAL STRUGGLE THAT HAD DEFINED HIM UP UNTIL NOW.
"SOMETHING MONSTROUS... SOMETHING WITH EYES THAT COULD PENETRATE EVERY DEFENSE HE COULD POSSIBLY CONSTRUCT... SOMETHING THAT KNEW HIM, INSIDE AND OUT.
"IT EMERGED FROM THE BLOOD AND MIST... TAUNTING HIM... DARING HIM TO CONFRONT THE DARKNESS THAT HE DID NOT WANT TO ACKNOWLEDGE.
"BUT INDEED IT WAS THERE. AND THIS... THING KNEW IT.
"ITS EXISTENCE SUGGESTED SOME SORT OF RECKONING YET TO COME... ONE THAT COULD NOT BE AVERTED OR AVOIDED.
"BUT NOT HERE. NOT NOW...
GUH--!
YOU'RE... AWAKE.
IT'S BEEN THREE DAYS...
Y-YOUR WIFE...
SHE IS WELL. SHE IS HEALED.
YOU DID IT.
I...
... I DID...?

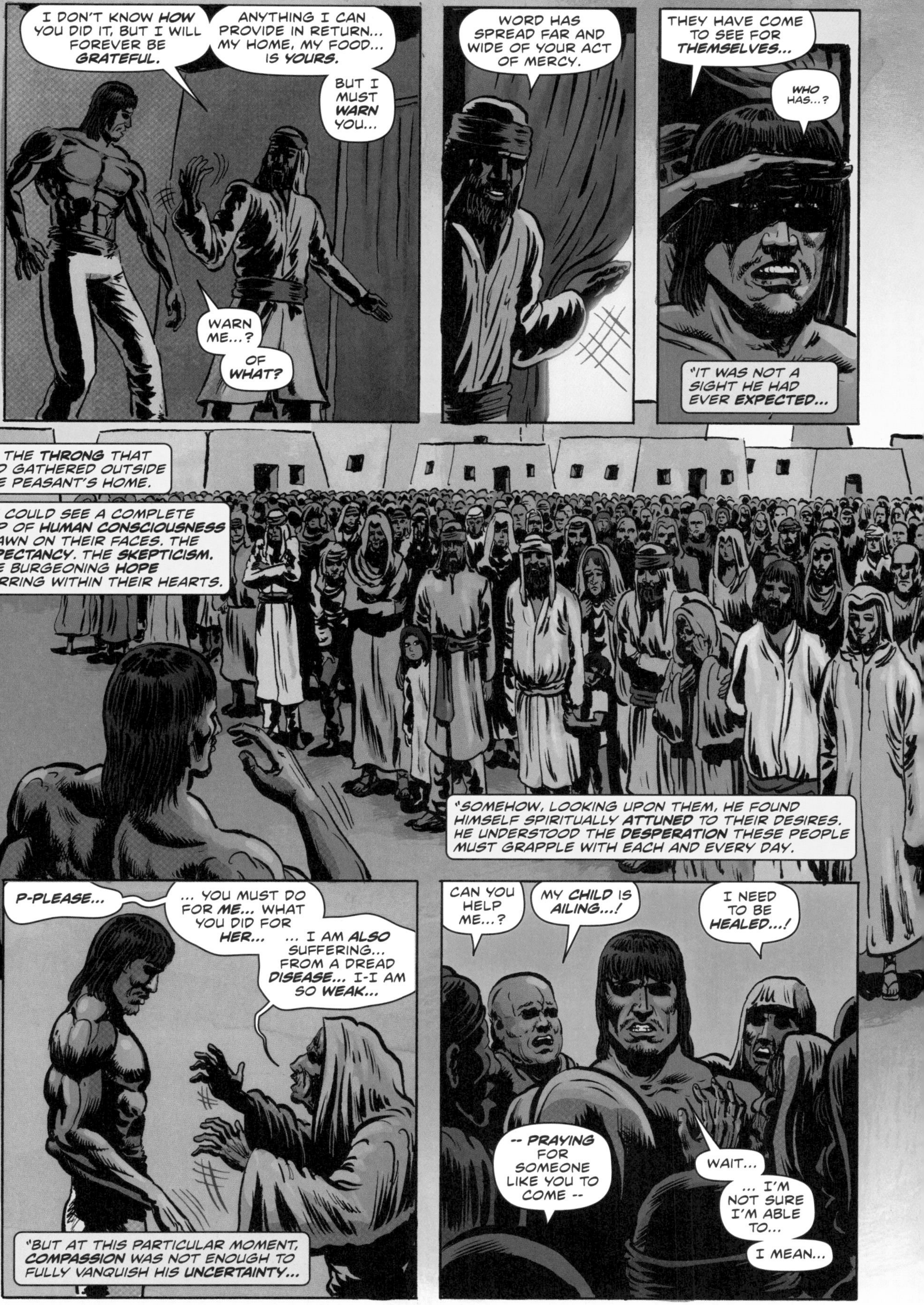
I DON'T KNOW HOW YOU DID IT, BUT I WILL FOREVER BE GRATEFUL.
ANYTHING I CAN PROVIDE IN RETURN... MY HOME, MY FOOD... IS YOURS.
BUT I MUST WARN YOU...
WARN ME...?
OF WHAT?
WORD HAS SPREAD FAR AND WIDE OF YOUR ACT OF MERCY.
THEY HAVE COME TO SEE FOR THEMSELVES...
WHO HAS...?
"IT WAS NOT A SIGHT HE HAD EVER EXPECTED...
"... THE THRONG THAT HAD GATHERED OUTSIDE THE PEASANT'S HOME.
"HE COULD SEE A COMPLETE MAP OF HUMAN CONSCIOUSNESS DRAWN ON THEIR FACES. THE EXPECTANCY. THE SKEPTICISM. THE BURGEONING HOPE STIRRING WITHIN THEIR HEARTS.
"SOMEHOW, LOOKING UPON THEM, HE FOUND HIMSELF SPIRITUALLY ATTUNED TO THEIR DESIRES. HE UNDERSTOOD THE DESPERATION THESE PEOPLE MUST GRAPPLE WITH EACH AND EVERY DAY.
P-PLEASE...
... YOU MUST DO FOR ME... WHAT YOU DID FOR HER...
... I AM ALSO SUFFERING... FROM A DREAD DISEASE... I-I AM SO WEAK...
"BUT AT THIS PARTICULAR MOMENT, COMPASSION WAS NOT ENOUGH TO FULLY VANQUISH HIS UNCERTAINTY...
CAN YOU HELP ME...?
MY CHILD IS AILING...!
I NEED TO BE HEALED...!
-- PRAYING FOR SOMEONE LIKE YOU TO COME --
WAIT...
... I'M NOT SURE I'M ABLE TO...
I MEAN...

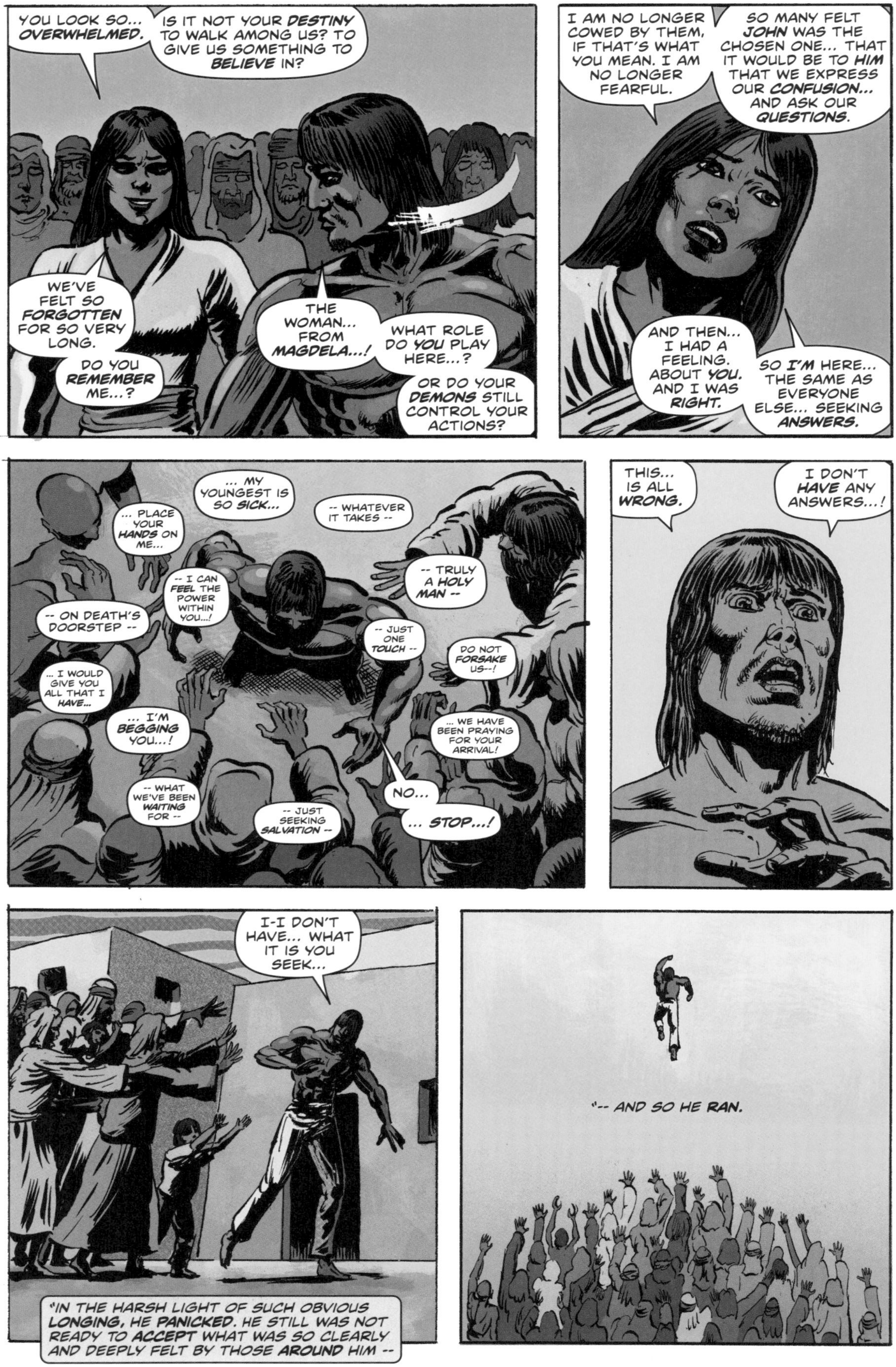
YOU LOOK SO... OVERWHELMED.
IS IT NOT YOUR DESTINY TO WALK AMONG US? TO GIVE US SOMETHING TO BELIEVE IN?
WE'VE FELT SO FORGOTTEN FOR SO VERY LONG.
DO YOU REMEMBER ME...?
THE WOMAN... FROM MAGDELA...!
WHAT ROLE DO YOU PLAY HERE...?
OR DO YOUR DEMONS STILL CONTROL YOUR ACTIONS?
I AM NO LONGER COWED BY THEM, IF THAT'S WHAT YOU MEAN. I AM NO LONGER FEARFUL.
SO MANY FELT JOHN WAS THE CHOSEN ONE... THAT IT WOULD BE TO HIM THAT WE EXPRESS OUR CONFUSION... AND ASK OUR QUESTIONS.
AND THEN... I HAD A FEELING. ABOUT YOU. AND I WAS RIGHT.
SO I'M HERE... THE SAME AS EVERYONE ELSE... SEEKING ANSWERS.
... MY YOUNGEST IS SO SICK...
-- WHATEVER IT TAKES --
... PLACE YOUR HANDS ON ME...
-- I CAN FEEL THE POWER WITHIN YOU...!
-- TRULY A HOLY MAN --
-- ON DEATH'S DOORSTEP --
-- JUST ONE TOUCH --
DO NOT FORSAKE US--!
... I WOULD GIVE YOU ALL THAT I HAVE...
... I'M BEGGING YOU...!
... WE HAVE BEEN PRAYING FOR YOUR ARRIVAL!
-- WHAT WE'VE BEEN WAITING FOR --
-- JUST SEEKING SALVATION --
NO...
... STOP...!
THIS... IS ALL WRONG.
I DON'T HAVE ANY ANSWERS...!
I-I DON'T HAVE... WHAT IT IS YOU SEEK...
"IN THE HARSH LIGHT OF SUCH OBVIOUS LONGING, HE PANICKED. HE STILL WAS NOT READY TO ACCEPT WHAT WAS SO CLEARLY AND DEEPLY FELT BY THOSE AROUND HIM --
"-- AND SO HE RAN.

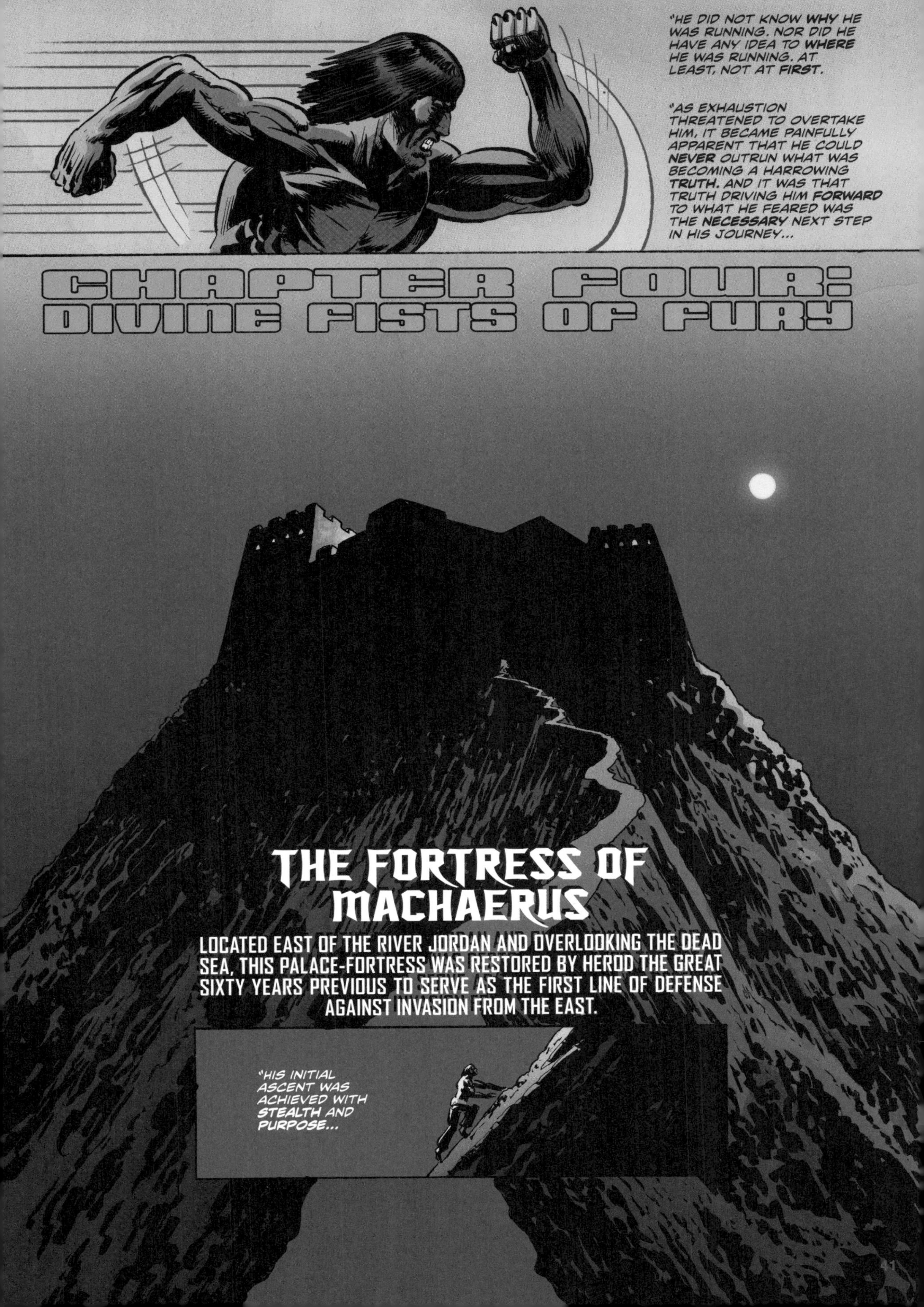

"HE DID NOT KNOW WHY HE WAS RUNNING. NOR DID HE HAVE ANY IDEA TO WHERE HE WAS RUNNING. AT LEAST, NOT AT FIRST.
"AS EXHAUSTION THREATENED TO OVERTAKE HIM, IT BECAME PAINFULLY APPARENT THAT HE COULD NEVER OUTRUN WHAT WAS BECOMING A HARROWING TRUTH. AND IT WAS THAT TRUTH DRIVING HIM FORWARD TO WHAT HE FEARED WAS THE NECESSARY NEXT STEP IN HIS JOURNEY...
CHAPTER FOUR: DIVINE FISTS OF FURY
THE FORTRESS OF MACHAERUS
LOCATED EAST OF THE RIVER JORDAN AND OVERLOOKING THE DEAD SEA, THIS PALACE-FORTRESS WAS RESTORED BY HEROD THE GREAT SIXTY YEARS PREVIOUS TO SERVE AS THE FIRST LINE OF DEFENSE AGAINST INVASION FROM THE EAST.
"HIS INITIAL ASCENT WAS ACHIEVED WITH STEALTH AND PURPOSE...

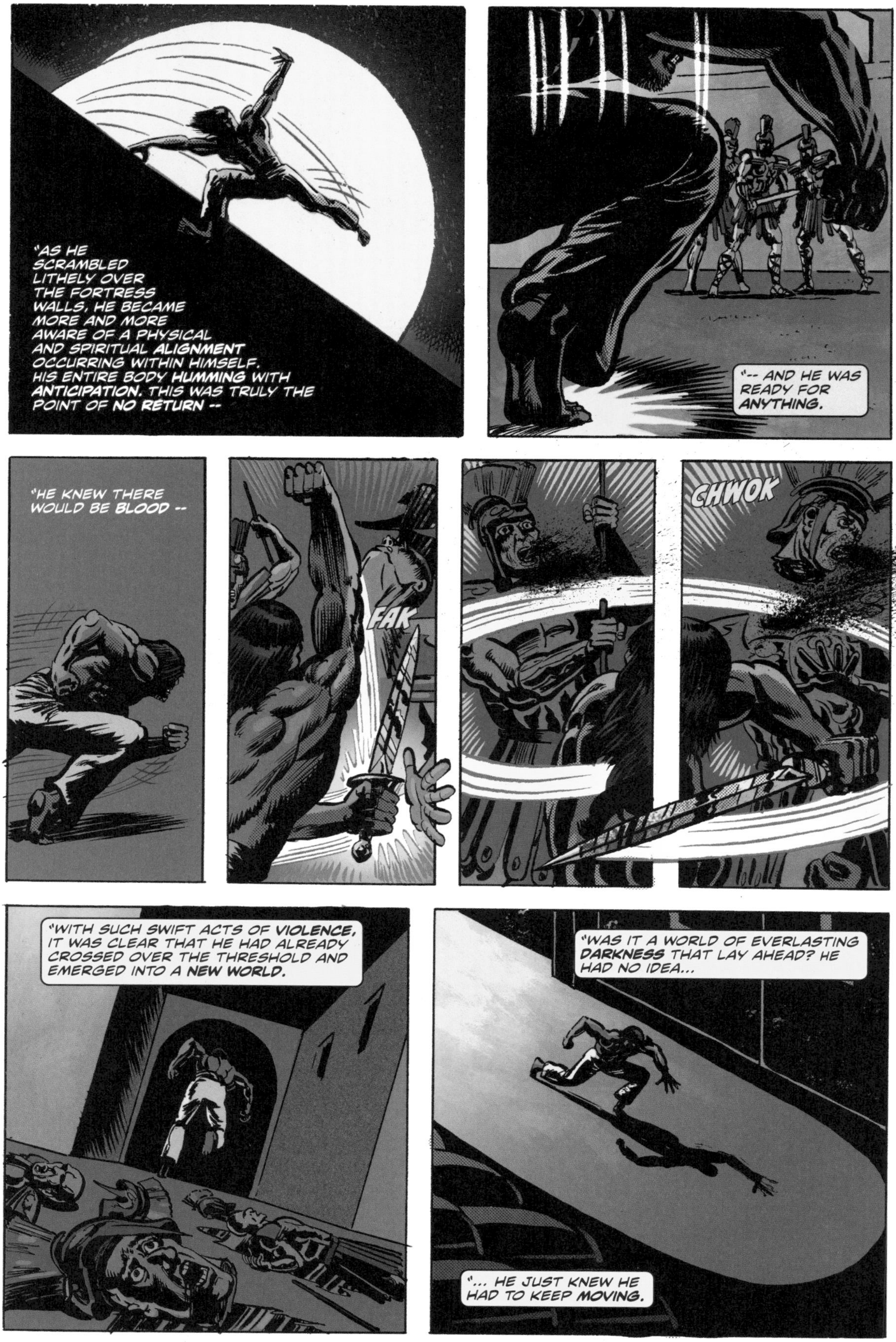
"AS HE SCRAMBLED LITHELY OVER THE FORTRESS WALLS, HE BECAME MORE AND MORE AWARE OF A PHYSICAL AND SPIRITUAL ALIGNMENT OCCURRING WITHIN HIMSELF. HIS ENTIRE BODY HUMMING WITH ANTICIPATION. THIS WAS TRULY THE POINT OF NO RETURN --
"-- AND HE WAS READY FOR ANYTHING.
"HE KNEW THERE WOULD BE BLOOD --
FAK
CHWOK
"WITH SUCH SWIFT ACTS OF VIOLENCE, IT WAS CLEAR THAT HE HAD ALREADY CROSSED OVER THE THRESHOLD AND EMERGED INTO A NEW WORLD.
"WAS IT A WORLD OF EVERLASTING DARKNESS THAT LAY AHEAD? HE HAD NO IDEA...
"... HE JUST KNEW HE HAD TO KEEP MOVING.

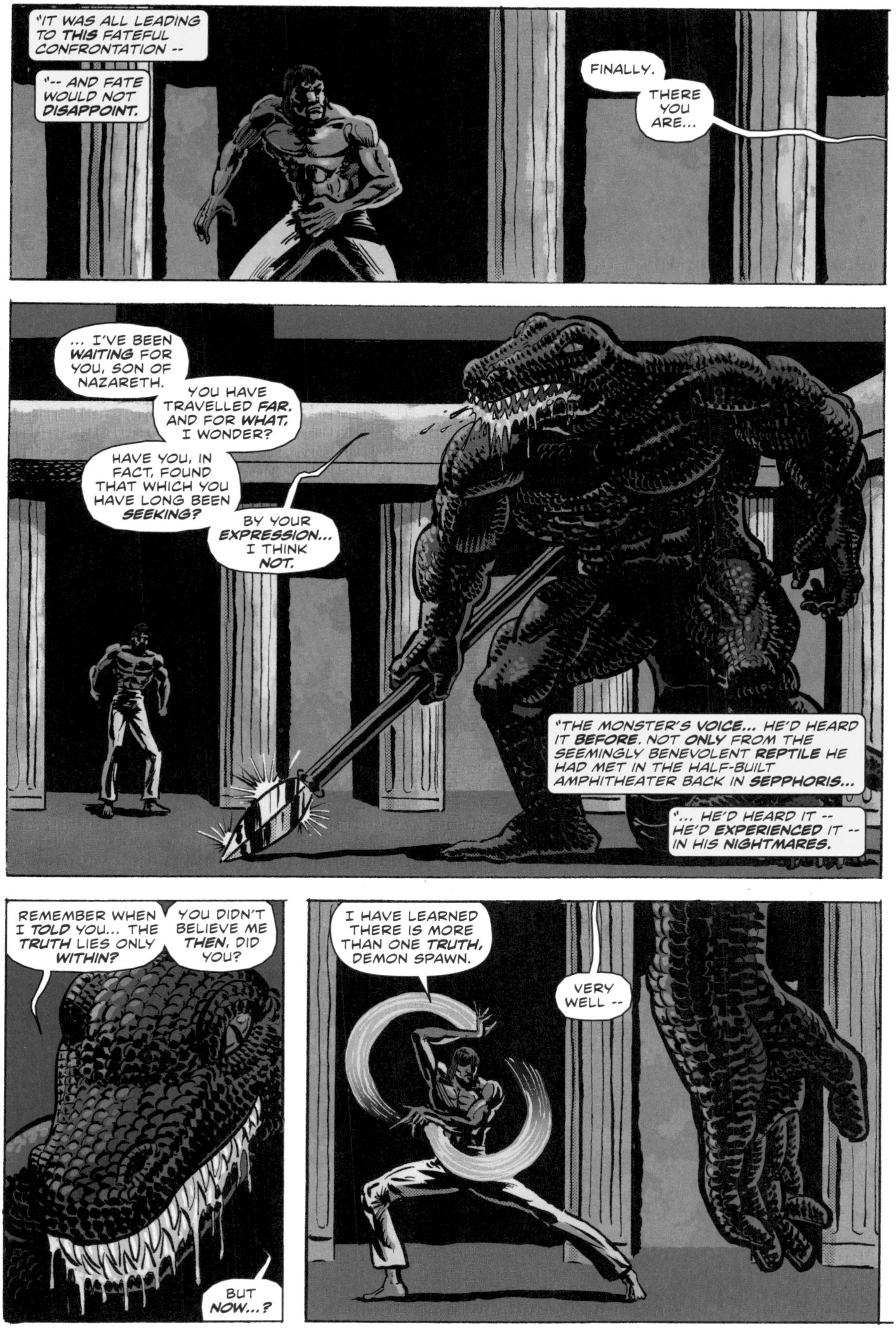

"IT WAS ALL LEADING TO THIS FATEFUL CONFRONTATION --
"-- AND FATE WOULD NOT DISAPPOINT.
FINALLY.
THERE YOU ARE...
... I'VE BEEN WAITING FOR YOU, SON OF NAZARETH.
YOU HAVE TRAVELLED FAR. AND FOR WHAT, I WONDER?
HAVE YOU, IN FACT, FOUND THAT WHICH YOU HAVE LONG BEEN SEEKING?
BY YOUR EXPRESSION... I THINK NOT.
"THE MONSTER'S VOICE... HE'D HEARD IT BEFORE. NOT ONLY FROM THE SEEMINGLY BENEVOLENT REPTILE HE HAD MET IN THE HALF-BUILT AMPHITHEATER BACK IN SEPPHORIS...
"... HE'D HEARD IT -- HE'D EXPERIENCED IT -- IN HIS NIGHTMARES.
REMEMBER WHEN I TOLD YOU... THE TRUTH LIES ONLY WITHIN?
YOU DIDN'T BELIEVE ME THEN, DID YOU?
BUT NOW...?
I HAVE LEARNED THERE IS MORE THAN ONE TRUTH, DEMON SPAWN.
VERY WELL --

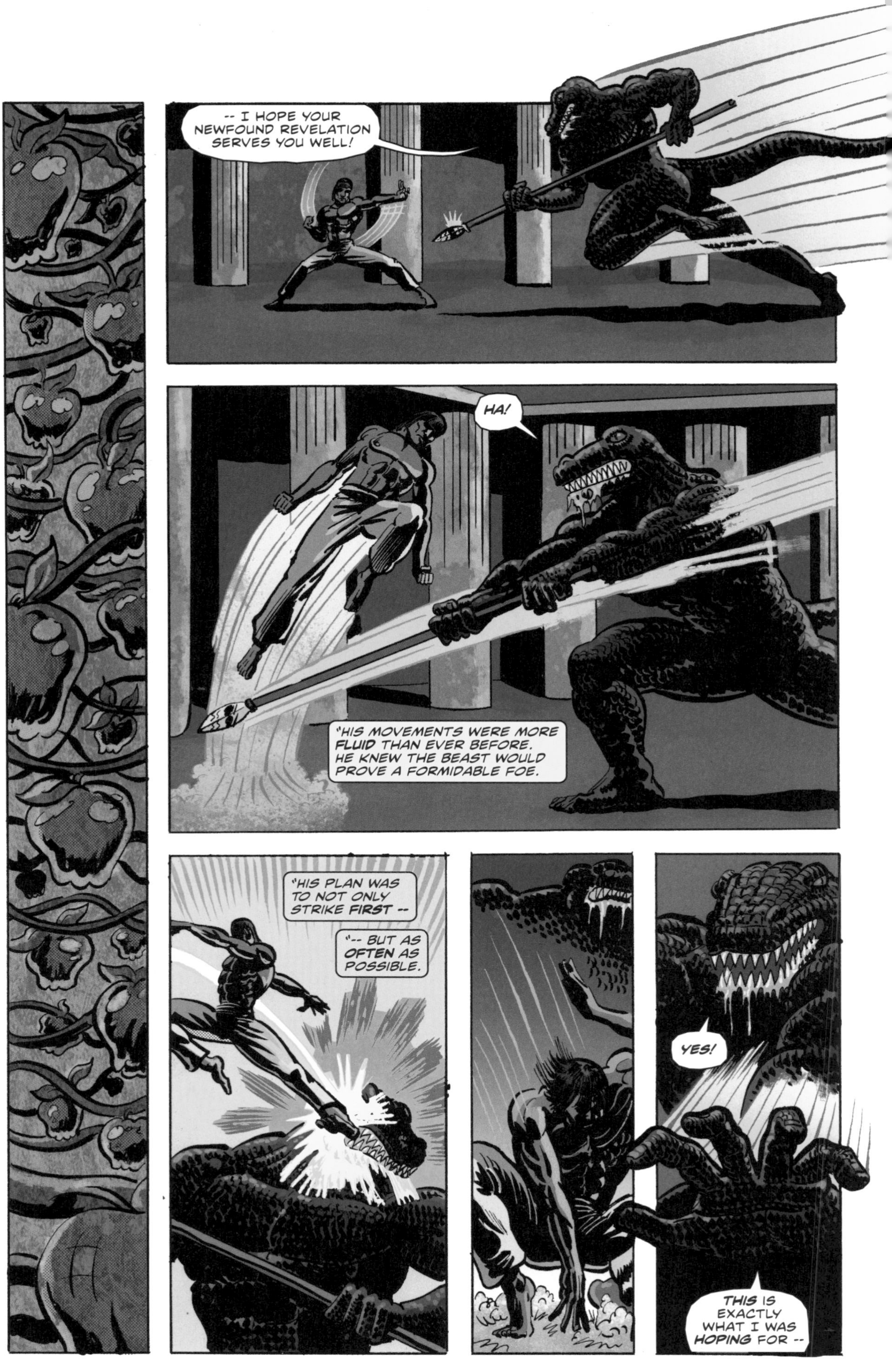
-- I HOPE YOUR NEWFOUND REVELATION SERVES YOU WELL!
HA!
"HIS MOVEMENTS WERE MORE **FLUID** THAN EVER BEFORE. HE KNEW THE BEAST WOULD PROVE A FORMIDABLE FOE.
"HIS PLAN WAS TO NOT ONLY STRIKE **FIRST** --
"-- BUT AS **OFTEN** AS POSSIBLE.
YES!
THIS IS EXACTLY WHAT I WAS **HOPING** FOR --

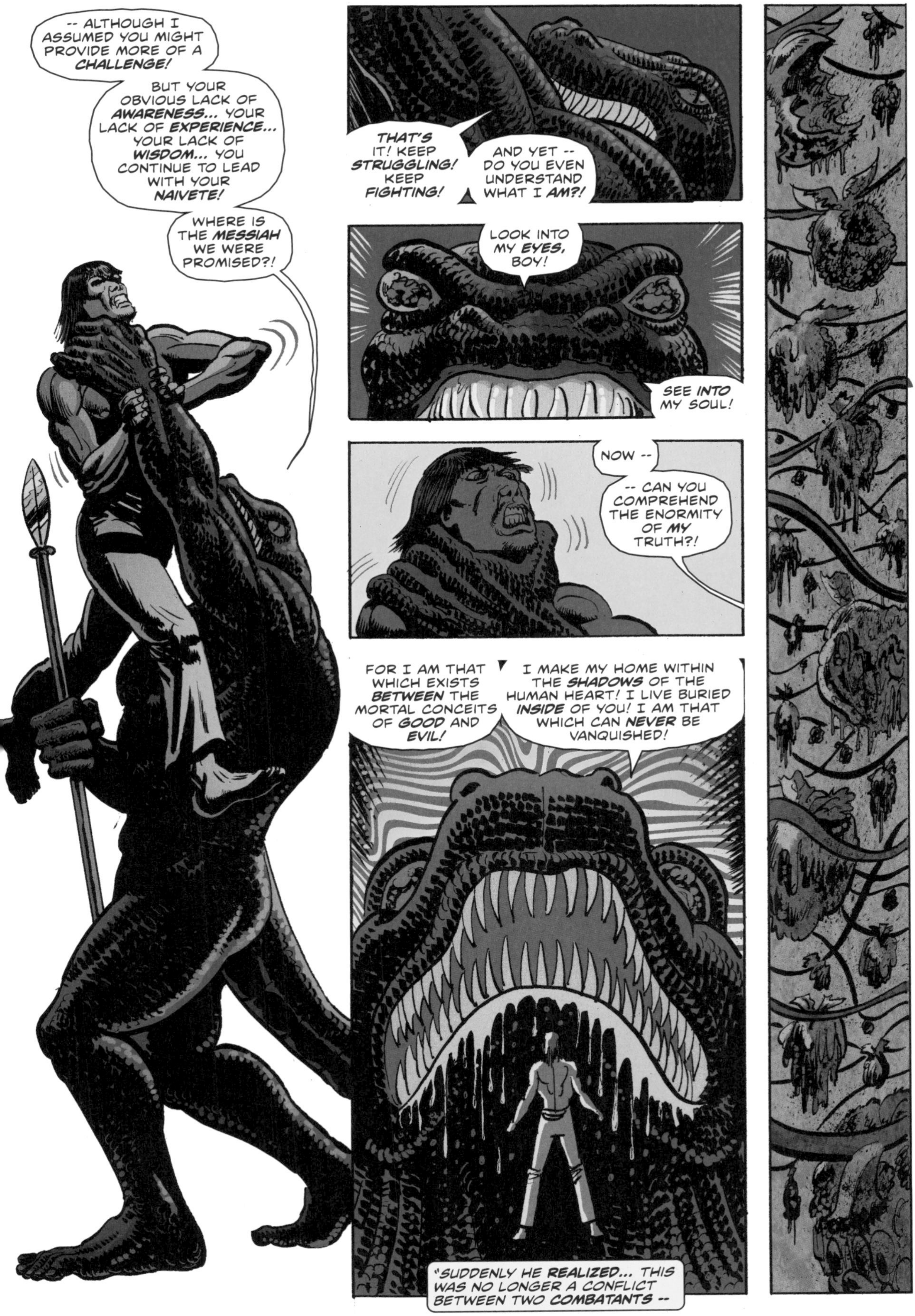
-- ALTHOUGH I ASSUMED YOU MIGHT PROVIDE MORE OF A CHALLENGE!
BUT YOUR OBVIOUS LACK OF AWARENESS... YOUR LACK OF EXPERIENCE... YOUR LACK OF WISDOM... YOU CONTINUE TO LEAD WITH YOUR NAIVETE!
WHERE IS THE MESSIAH WE WERE PROMISED?!
THAT'S IT! KEEP STRUGGLING! KEEP FIGHTING!
AND YET -- DO YOU EVEN UNDERSTAND WHAT I AM?!
LOOK INTO MY EYES, BOY!
SEE INTO MY SOUL!
NOW --
-- CAN YOU COMPREHEND THE ENORMITY OF MY TRUTH?!
FOR I AM THAT WHICH EXISTS BETWEEN THE MORTAL CONCEITS OF GOOD AND EVIL!
I MAKE MY HOME WITHIN THE SHADOWS OF THE HUMAN HEART! I LIVE BURIED INSIDE OF YOU! I AM THAT WHICH CAN NEVER BE VANQUISHED!
"SUDDENLY HE REALIZED... THIS WAS NO LONGER A CONFLICT BETWEEN TWO COMBATANTS --

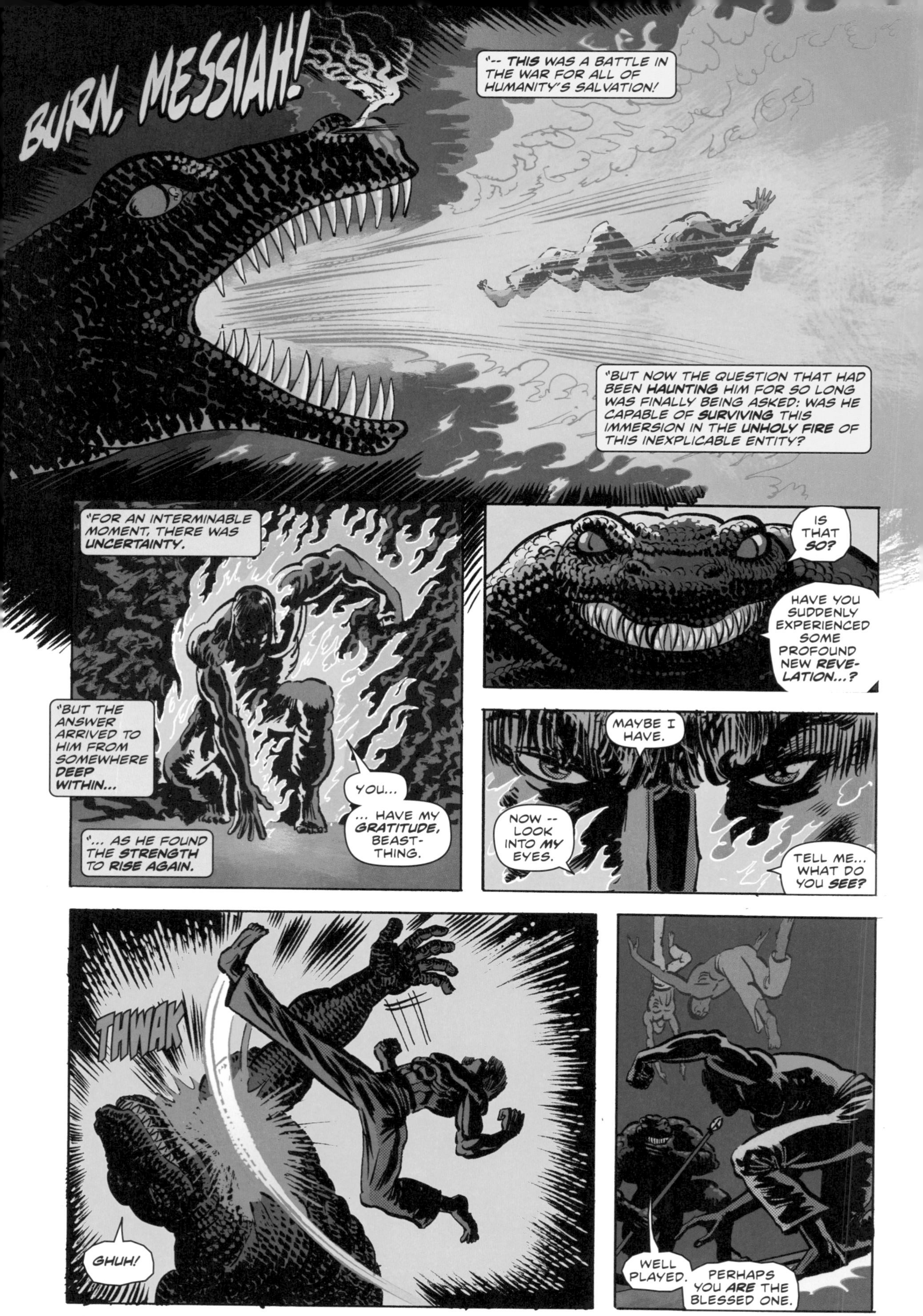
BURN, MESSIAH!
"-- THIS WAS A BATTLE IN THE WAR FOR ALL OF HUMANITY'S SALVATION!
"BUT NOW THE QUESTION THAT HAD BEEN HAUNTING HIM FOR SO LONG WAS FINALLY BEING ASKED: WAS HE CAPABLE OF SURVIVING THIS IMMERSION IN THE UNHOLY FIRE OF THIS INEXPLICABLE ENTITY?
"FOR AN INTERMINABLE MOMENT, THERE WAS UNCERTAINTY.
"BUT THE ANSWER ARRIVED TO HIM FROM SOMEWHERE DEEP WITHIN...
"... AS HE FOUND THE STRENGTH TO RISE AGAIN.
YOU...
... HAVE MY GRATITUDE, BEAST-THING.
IS THAT SO?
HAVE YOU SUDDENLY EXPERIENCED SOME PROFOUND NEW REVE-LATION...?
MAYBE I HAVE.
NOW -- LOOK INTO MY EYES.
TELL ME... WHAT DO YOU SEE?
THWAK
GHUH!
WELL PLAYED.
PERHAPS YOU ARE THE BLESSED ONE.

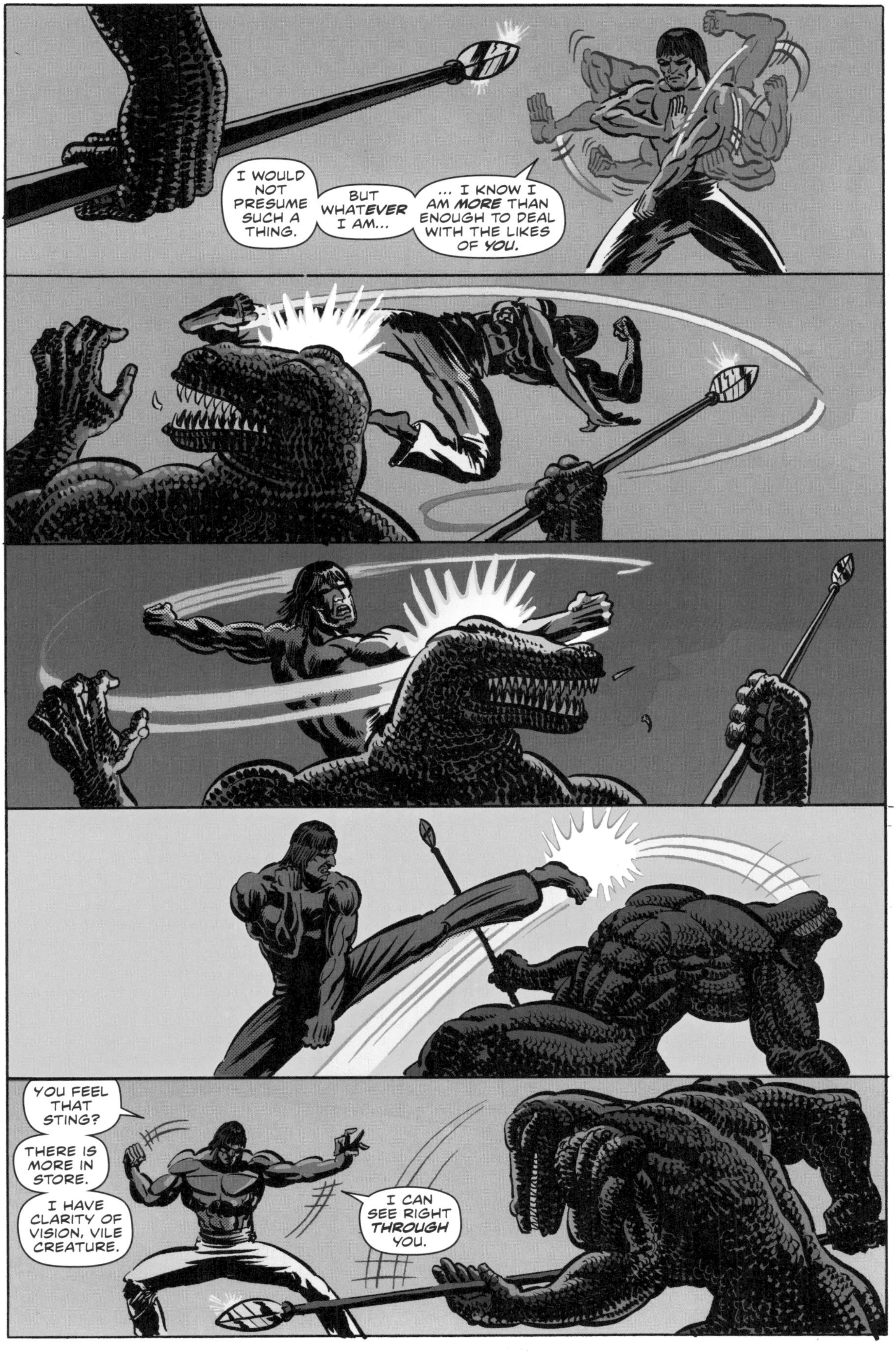
I WOULD NOT PRESUME SUCH A THING.
BUT WHATEVER I AM...
... I KNOW I AM MORE THAN ENOUGH TO DEAL WITH THE LIKES OF YOU.
YOU FEEL THAT STING?
THERE IS MORE IN STORE.
I HAVE CLARITY OF VISION, VILE CREATURE.
I CAN SEE RIGHT THROUGH YOU.

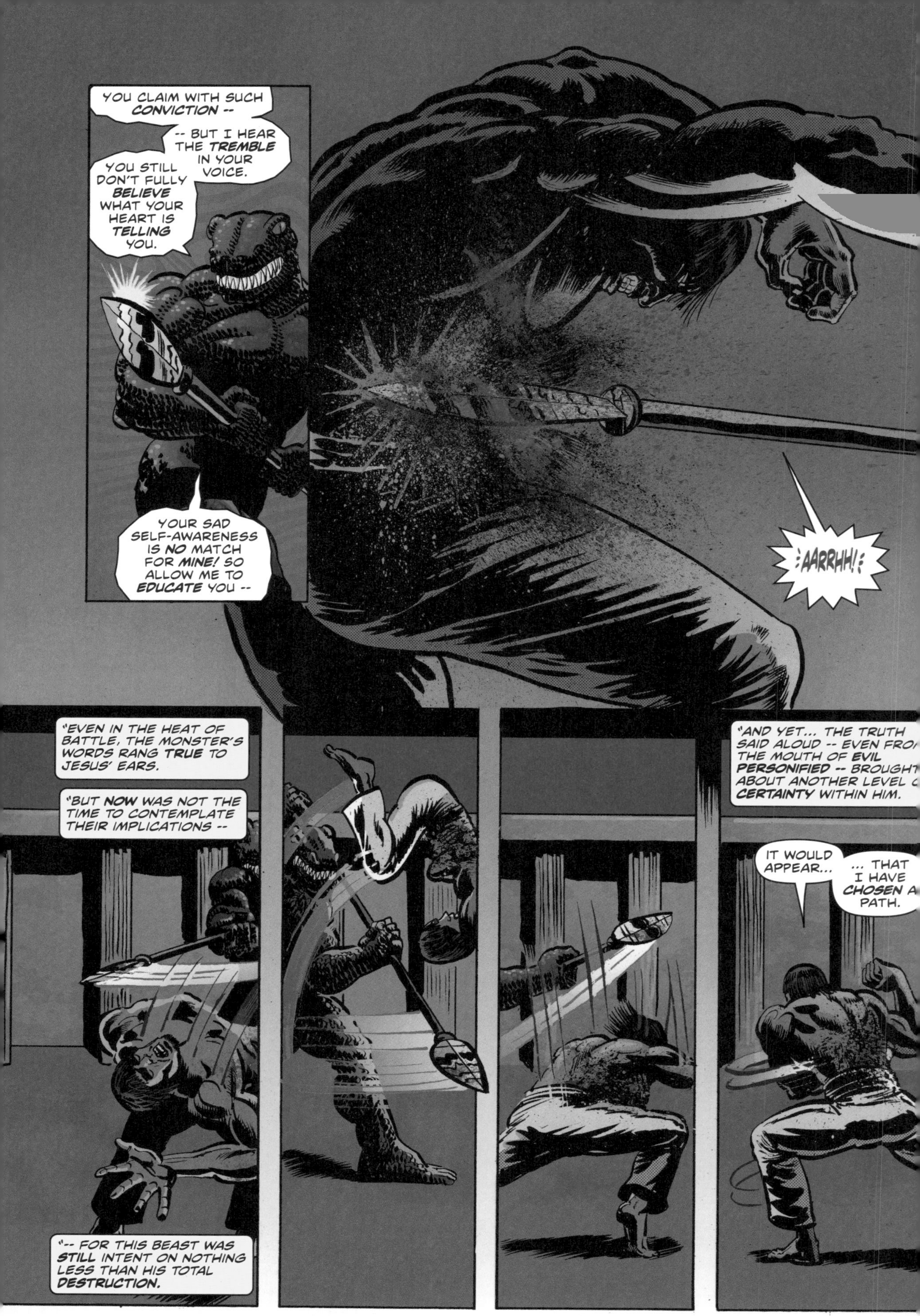
YOU CLAIM WITH SUCH CONVICTION --
-- BUT I HEAR THE TREMBLE IN YOUR VOICE.
YOU STILL DON'T FULLY BELIEVE WHAT YOUR HEART IS TELLING YOU.
YOUR SAD SELF-AWARENESS IS NO MATCH FOR MINE! SO ALLOW ME TO EDUCATE YOU --
AARRHH!
"EVEN IN THE HEAT OF BATTLE, THE MONSTER'S WORDS RANG TRUE TO JESUS' EARS.
"BUT NOW WAS NOT THE TIME TO CONTEMPLATE THEIR IMPLICATIONS --
"-- FOR THIS BEAST WAS STILL INTENT ON NOTHING LESS THAN HIS TOTAL DESTRUCTION.
"AND YET... THE TRUTH SAID ALOUD -- EVEN FRO THE MOUTH OF EVIL PERSONIFIED -- BROUGHT ABOUT ANOTHER LEVEL O CERTAINTY WITHIN HIM.
IT WOULD APPEAR...
... THAT I HAVE CHOSEN A PATH.

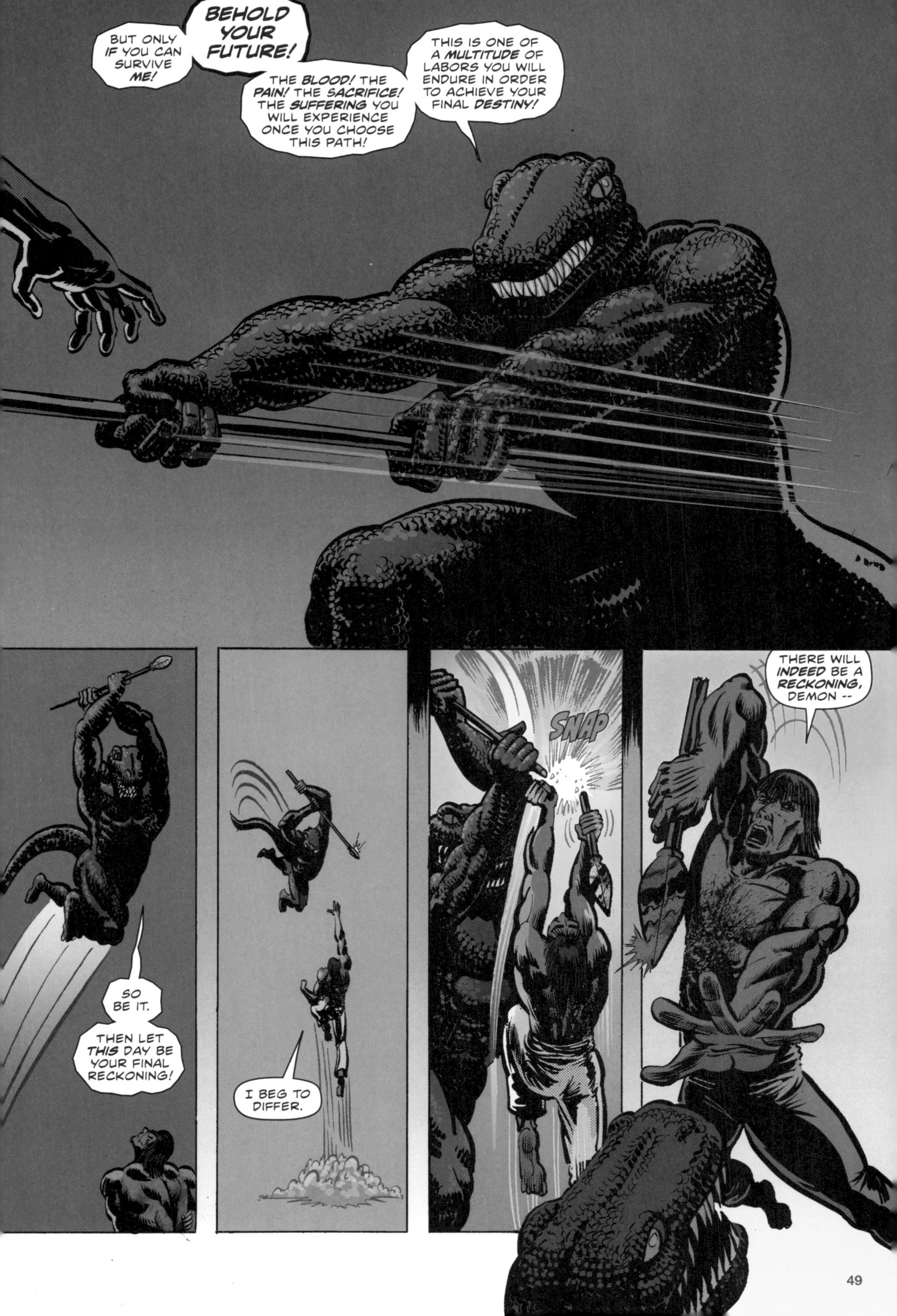
BUT ONLY IF YOU CAN SURVIVE ME!
BEHOLD YOUR FUTURE!
THE BLOOD! THE PAIN! THE SACRIFICE! THE SUFFERING YOU WILL EXPERIENCE ONCE YOU CHOOSE THIS PATH!
THIS IS ONE OF A MULTITUDE OF LABORS YOU WILL ENDURE IN ORDER TO ACHIEVE YOUR FINAL DESTINY!
SO BE IT.
THEN LET THIS DAY BE YOUR FINAL RECKONING!
I BEG TO DIFFER.
SNAP
THERE WILL INDEED BE A RECKONING, DEMON --

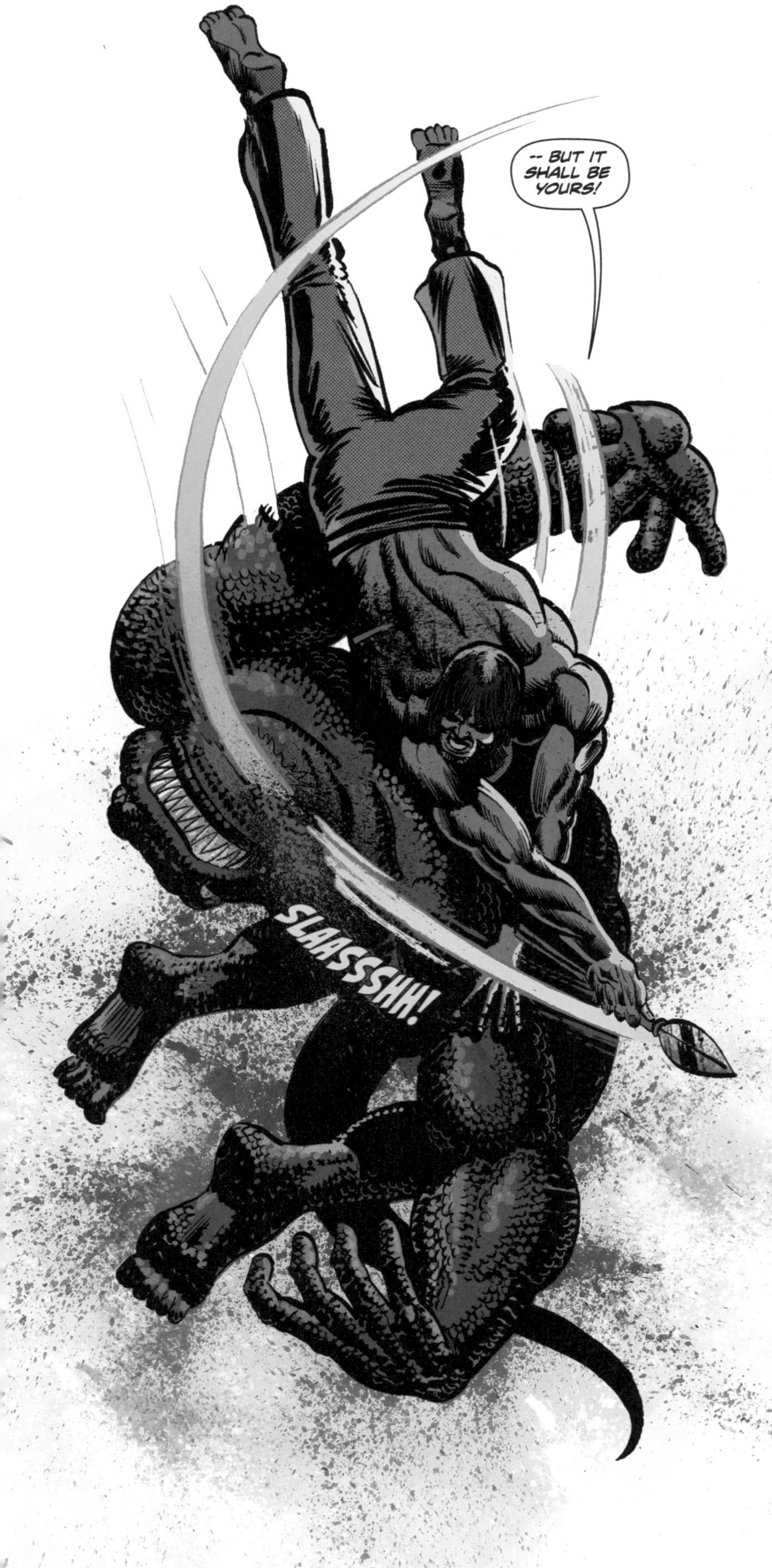
-- BUT IT SHALL BE YOURS!
SLAASSSHH!

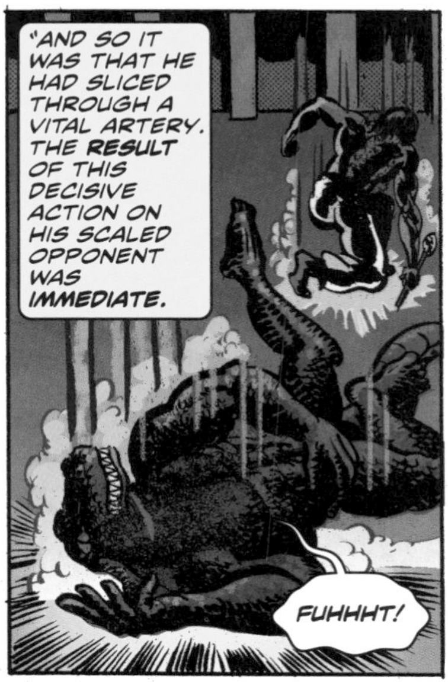
"AND SO IT WAS THAT HE HAD SLICED THROUGH A VITAL ARTERY. THE RESULT OF THIS DECISIVE ACTION ON HIS SCALED OPPONENT WAS IMMEDIATE.
FUHHHT!

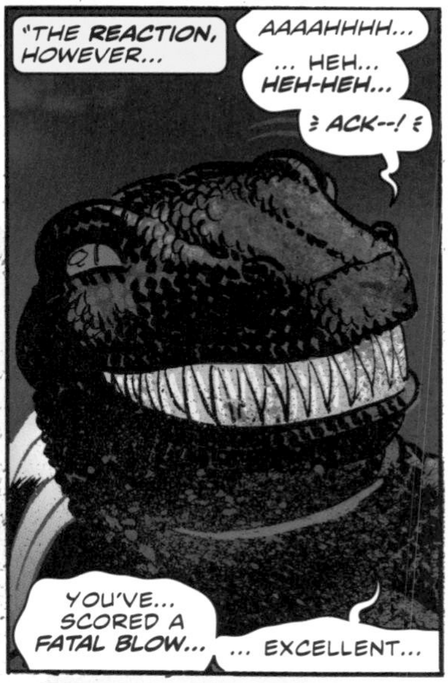
"THE REACTION, HOWEVER...
AAAAHHHH... ... HEH... HEH-HEH...
ACK--!
YOU'VE... SCORED A FATAL BLOW...
... EXCELLENT...

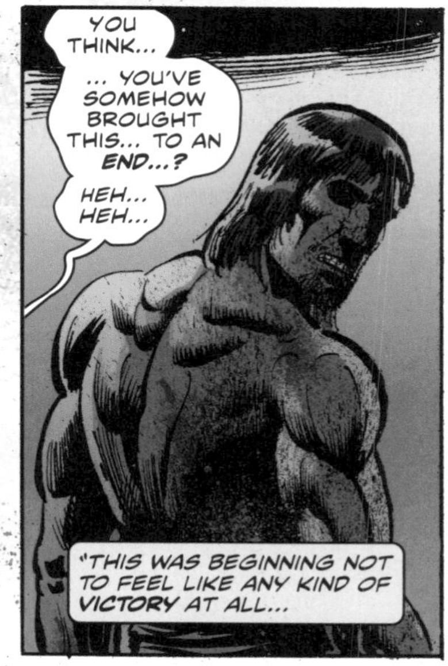
YOU THINK...
... YOU'VE SOMEHOW BROUGHT THIS... TO AN END...?
HEH... HEH...
"THIS WAS BEGINNING NOT TO FEEL LIKE ANY KIND OF VICTORY AT ALL...

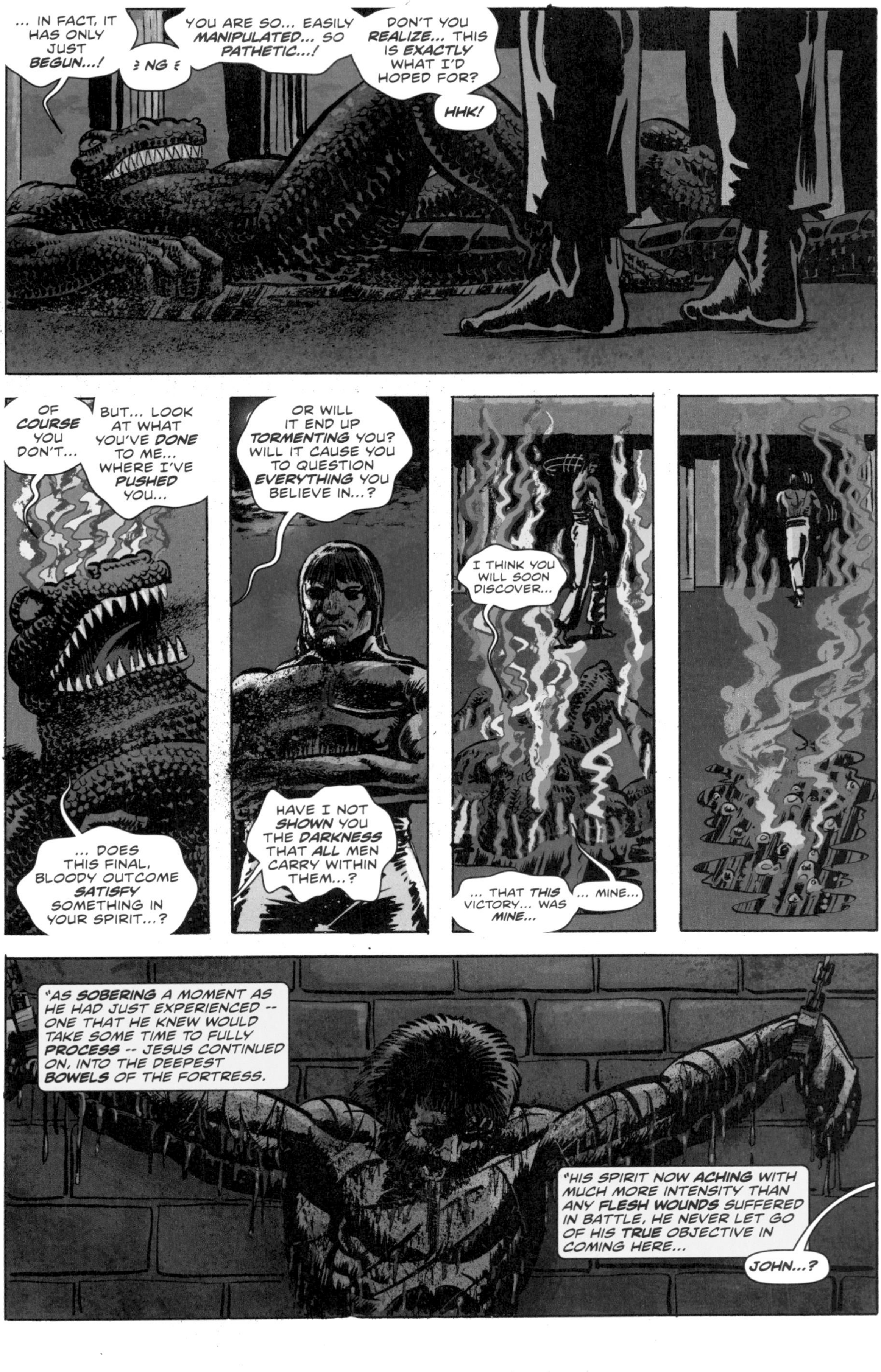
... IN FACT, IT HAS ONLY JUST BEGUN...!
NG
YOU ARE SO... EASILY MANIPULATED... SO PATHETIC...!
DON'T YOU REALIZE... THIS IS EXACTLY WHAT I'D HOPED FOR?
HHK!
OF COURSE YOU DON'T...
BUT... LOOK AT WHAT YOU'VE DONE TO ME... WHERE I'VE PUSHED YOU...
... DOES THIS FINAL, BLOODY OUTCOME SATISFY SOMETHING IN YOUR SPIRIT...?
OR WILL IT END UP TORMENTING YOU? WILL IT CAUSE YOU TO QUESTION EVERYTHING YOU BELIEVE IN...?
HAVE I NOT SHOWN YOU THE DARKNESS THAT ALL MEN CARRY WITHIN THEM...?
I THINK YOU WILL SOON DISCOVER...
... THAT THIS VICTORY... WAS MINE...
... MINE...
"AS SOBERING A MOMENT AS HE HAD JUST EXPERIENCED -- ONE THAT HE KNEW WOULD TAKE SOME TIME TO FULLY PROCESS -- JESUS CONTINUED ON, INTO THE DEEPEST BOWELS OF THE FORTRESS.
"HIS SPIRIT NOW ACHING WITH MUCH MORE INTENSITY THAN ANY FLESH WOUNDS SUFFERED IN BATTLE, HE NEVER LET GO OF HIS TRUE OBJECTIVE IN COMING HERE...
JOHN...?

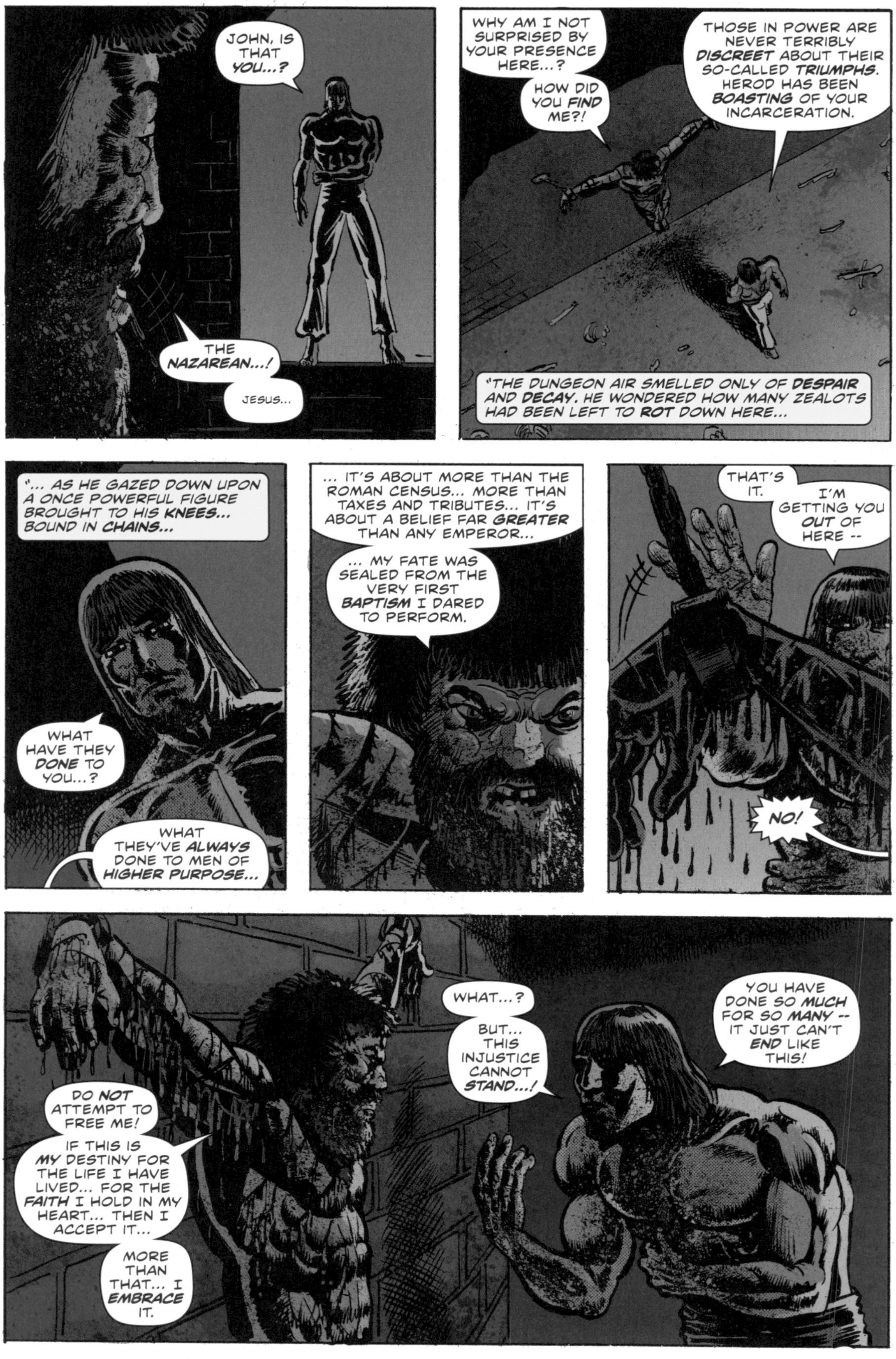
JOHN, IS THAT YOU...?
THE NAZAREAN...!
JESUS...
WHY AM I NOT SURPRISED BY YOUR PRESENCE HERE...?
HOW DID YOU FIND ME?!
THOSE IN POWER ARE NEVER TERRIBLY DISCREET ABOUT THEIR SO-CALLED TRIUMPHS. HEROD HAS BEEN BOASTING OF YOUR INCARCERATION.
"THE DUNGEON AIR SMELLED ONLY OF DESPAIR AND DECAY. HE WONDERED HOW MANY ZEALOTS HAD BEEN LEFT TO ROT DOWN HERE...
"... AS HE GAZED DOWN UPON A ONCE POWERFUL FIGURE BROUGHT TO HIS KNEES... BOUND IN CHAINS...
WHAT HAVE THEY DONE TO YOU...?
WHAT THEY'VE ALWAYS DONE TO MEN OF HIGHER PURPOSE...
... IT'S ABOUT MORE THAN THE ROMAN CENSUS... MORE THAN TAXES AND TRIBUTES... IT'S ABOUT A BELIEF FAR GREATER THAN ANY EMPEROR...
... MY FATE WAS SEALED FROM THE VERY FIRST BAPTISM I DARED TO PERFORM.
THAT'S IT.
I'M GETTING YOU OUT OF HERE --
NO!
DO NOT ATTEMPT TO FREE ME!
IF THIS IS MY DESTINY FOR THE LIFE I HAVE LIVED... FOR THE FAITH I HOLD IN MY HEART... THEN I ACCEPT IT...
MORE THAN THAT... I EMBRACE IT.
WHAT...?
BUT... THIS INJUSTICE CANNOT STAND...!
YOU HAVE DONE SO MUCH FOR SO MANY -- IT JUST CAN'T END LIKE THIS!

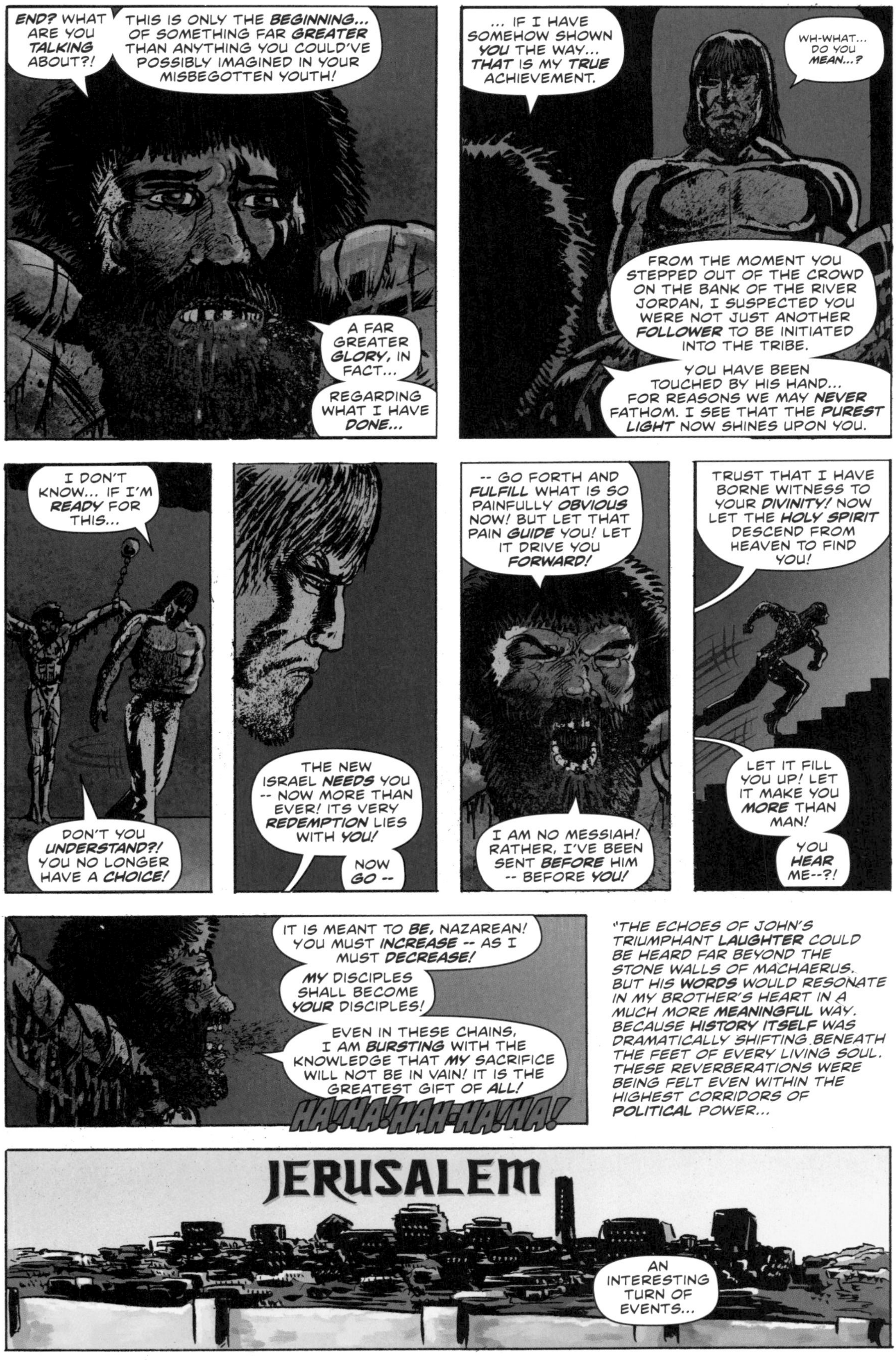
END? WHAT ARE YOU TALKING ABOUT?!
THIS IS ONLY THE BEGINNING... OF SOMETHING FAR GREATER THAN ANYTHING YOU COULD'VE POSSIBLY IMAGINED IN YOUR MISBEGOTTEN YOUTH!
A FAR GREATER GLORY, IN FACT...
REGARDING WHAT I HAVE DONE...
... IF I HAVE SOMEHOW SHOWN YOU THE WAY... THAT IS MY TRUE ACHIEVEMENT.
WH-WHAT... DO YOU MEAN...?
FROM THE MOMENT YOU STEPPED OUT OF THE CROWD ON THE BANK OF THE RIVER JORDAN, I SUSPECTED YOU WERE NOT JUST ANOTHER FOLLOWER TO BE INITIATED INTO THE TRIBE.
YOU HAVE BEEN TOUCHED BY HIS HAND... FOR REASONS WE MAY NEVER FATHOM. I SEE THAT THE PUREST LIGHT NOW SHINES UPON YOU.
I DON'T KNOW... IF I'M READY FOR THIS...
DON'T YOU UNDERSTAND?! YOU NO LONGER HAVE A CHOICE!
THE NEW ISRAEL NEEDS YOU -- NOW MORE THAN EVER! ITS VERY REDEMPTION LIES WITH YOU!
NOW GO --
-- GO FORTH AND FULFILL WHAT IS SO PAINFULLY OBVIOUS NOW! BUT LET THAT PAIN GUIDE YOU! LET IT DRIVE YOU FORWARD!
I AM NO MESSIAH! RATHER, I'VE BEEN SENT BEFORE HIM -- BEFORE YOU!
TRUST THAT I HAVE BORNE WITNESS TO YOUR DIVINITY! NOW LET THE HOLY SPIRIT DESCEND FROM HEAVEN TO FIND YOU!
LET IT FILL YOU UP! LET IT MAKE YOU MORE THAN MAN!
YOU HEAR ME--?!
IT IS MEANT TO BE, NAZAREAN! YOU MUST INCREASE -- AS I MUST DECREASE!
MY DISCIPLES SHALL BECOME YOUR DISCIPLES!
EVEN IN THESE CHAINS, I AM BURSTING WITH THE KNOWLEDGE THAT MY SACRIFICE WILL NOT BE IN VAIN! IT IS THE GREATEST GIFT OF ALL!
HA! HA! HAH-HA! HA!
"THE ECHOES OF JOHN'S TRIUMPHANT LAUGHTER COULD BE HEARD FAR BEYOND THE STONE WALLS OF MACHAERUS. BUT HIS WORDS WOULD RESONATE IN MY BROTHER'S HEART IN A MUCH MORE MEANINGFUL WAY. BECAUSE HISTORY ITSELF WAS DRAMATICALLY SHIFTING BENEATH THE FEET OF EVERY LIVING SOUL. THESE REVERBERATIONS WERE BEING FELT EVEN WITHIN THE HIGHEST CORRIDORS OF POLITICAL POWER...
JERUSALEM
AN INTERESTING TURN OF EVENTS...

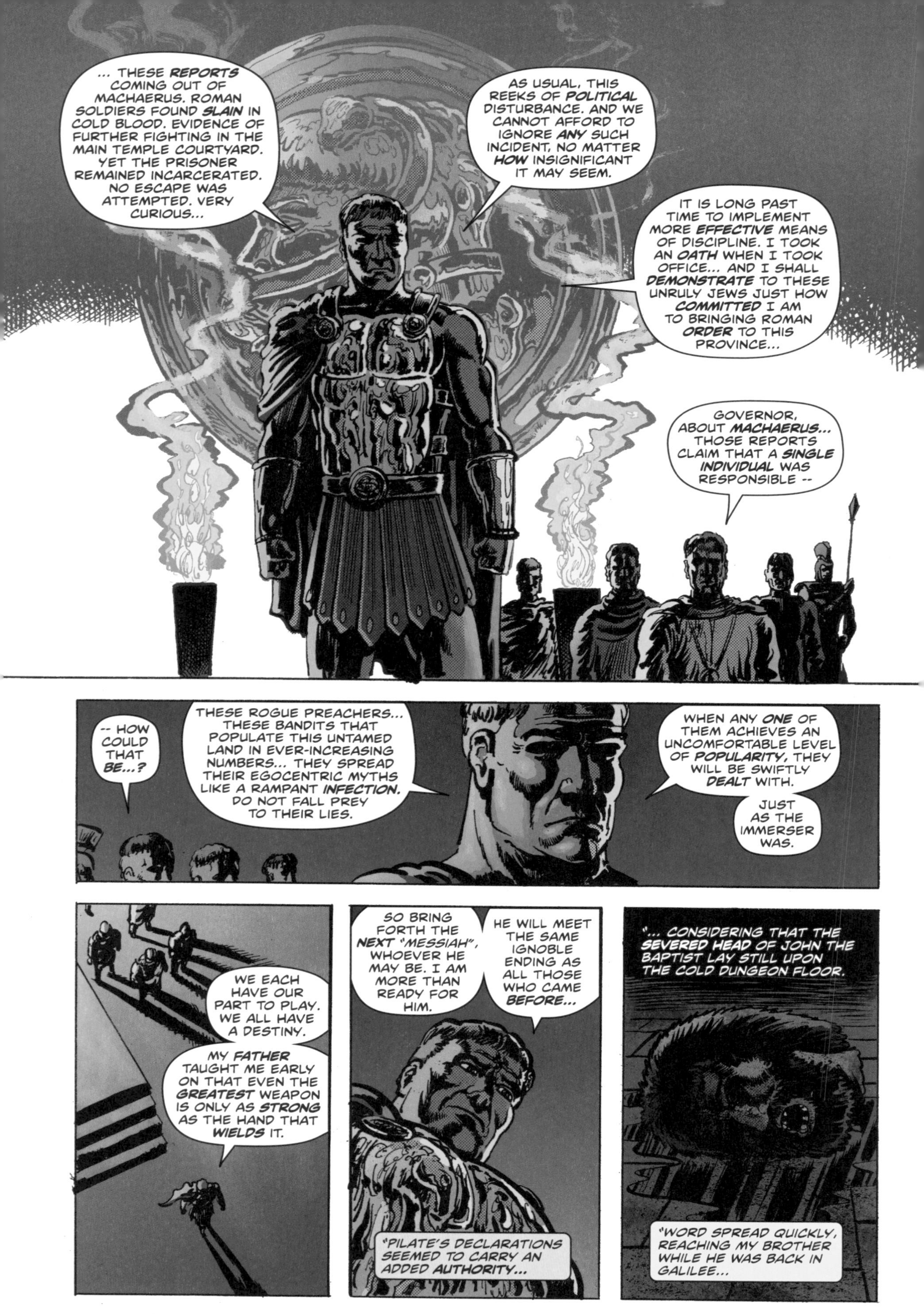
... THESE REPORTS COMING OUT OF MACHAERUS. ROMAN SOLDIERS FOUND SLAIN IN COLD BLOOD. EVIDENCE OF FURTHER FIGHTING IN THE MAIN TEMPLE COURTYARD. YET THE PRISONER REMAINED INCARCERATED. NO ESCAPE WAS ATTEMPTED. VERY CURIOUS...
AS USUAL, THIS REEKS OF POLITICAL DISTURBANCE. AND WE CANNOT AFFORD TO IGNORE ANY SUCH INCIDENT, NO MATTER HOW INSIGNIFICANT IT MAY SEEM.
IT IS LONG PAST TIME TO IMPLEMENT MORE EFFECTIVE MEANS OF DISCIPLINE. I TOOK AN OATH WHEN I TOOK OFFICE... AND I SHALL DEMONSTRATE TO THESE UNRULY JEWS JUST HOW COMMITTED I AM TO BRINGING ROMAN ORDER TO THIS PROVINCE...
GOVERNOR, ABOUT MACHAERUS... THOSE REPORTS CLAIM THAT A SINGLE INDIVIDUAL WAS RESPONSIBLE --
-- HOW COULD THAT BE...?
THESE ROGUE PREACHERS... THESE BANDITS THAT POPULATE THIS UNTAMED LAND IN EVER-INCREASING NUMBERS... THEY SPREAD THEIR EGOCENTRIC MYTHS LIKE A RAMPANT INFECTION. DO NOT FALL PREY TO THEIR LIES.
WHEN ANY ONE OF THEM ACHIEVES AN UNCOMFORTABLE LEVEL OF POPULARITY, THEY WILL BE SWIFTLY DEALT WITH.
JUST AS THE IMMERSER WAS.
WE EACH HAVE OUR PART TO PLAY. WE ALL HAVE A DESTINY.
MY FATHER TAUGHT ME EARLY ON THAT EVEN THE GREATEST WEAPON IS ONLY AS STRONG AS THE HAND THAT WIELDS IT.
SO BRING FORTH THE NEXT "MESSIAH", WHOEVER HE MAY BE. I AM MORE THAN READY FOR HIM.
HE WILL MEET THE SAME IGNOBLE ENDING AS ALL THOSE WHO CAME BEFORE...
"PILATE'S DECLARATIONS SEEMED TO CARRY AN ADDED AUTHORITY...
"... CONSIDERING THAT THE SEVERED HEAD OF JOHN THE BAPTIST LAY STILL UPON THE COLD DUNGEON FLOOR.
"WORD SPREAD QUICKLY, REACHING MY BROTHER WHILE HE WAS BACK IN GALILEE...

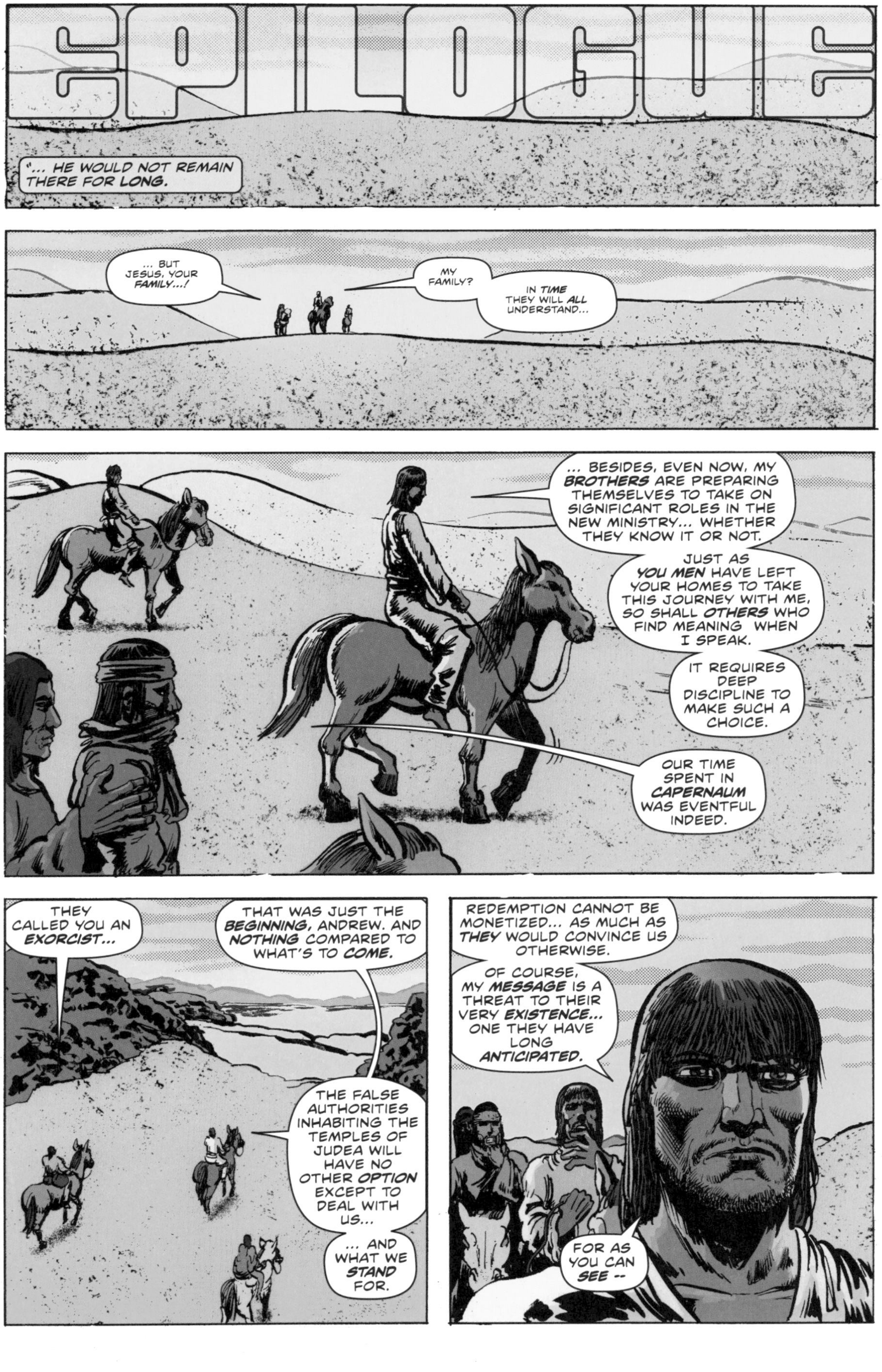
EPILOGUE
"... HE WOULD NOT REMAIN THERE FOR LONG.
... BUT JESUS, YOUR FAMILY...!
MY FAMILY?
IN TIME THEY WILL ALL UNDERSTAND...
... BESIDES, EVEN NOW, MY BROTHERS ARE PREPARING THEMSELVES TO TAKE ON SIGNIFICANT ROLES IN THE NEW MINISTRY... WHETHER THEY KNOW IT OR NOT.
JUST AS YOU MEN HAVE LEFT YOUR HOMES TO TAKE THIS JOURNEY WITH ME, SO SHALL OTHERS WHO FIND MEANING WHEN I SPEAK.
IT REQUIRES DEEP DISCIPLINE TO MAKE SUCH A CHOICE.
OUR TIME SPENT IN CAPERNAUM WAS EVENTFUL INDEED.
THEY CALLED YOU AN EXORCIST...
THAT WAS JUST THE BEGINNING, ANDREW. AND NOTHING COMPARED TO WHAT'S TO COME.
THE FALSE AUTHORITIES INHABITING THE TEMPLES OF JUDEA WILL HAVE NO OTHER OPTION EXCEPT TO DEAL WITH US...
... AND WHAT WE STAND FOR.
REDEMPTION CANNOT BE MONETIZED... AS MUCH AS THEY WOULD CONVINCE US OTHERWISE.
OF COURSE, MY MESSAGE IS A THREAT TO THEIR VERY EXISTENCE... ONE THEY HAVE LONG ANTICIPATED.
FOR AS YOU CAN SEE --

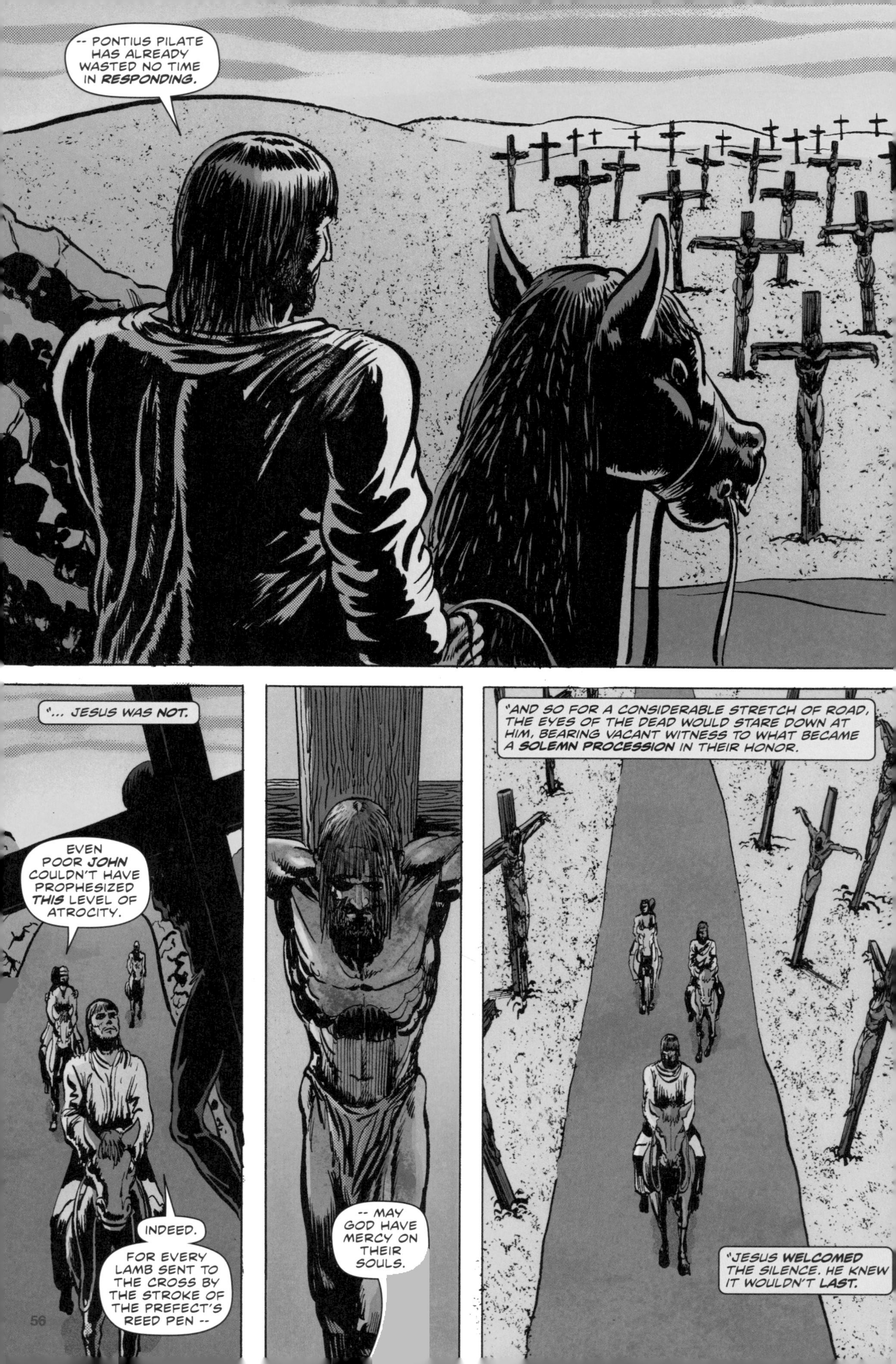
-- PONTIUS PILATE HAS ALREADY WASTED NO TIME IN **RESPONDING.**
"... JESUS WAS **NOT.**
EVEN POOR **JOHN** COULDN'T HAVE PROPHESIZED **THIS** LEVEL OF ATROCITY.
INDEED.
FOR EVERY LAMB SENT TO THE CROSS BY THE STROKE OF THE PREFECT'S REED PEN --
-- MAY GOD HAVE MERCY ON THEIR SOULS.
"AND SO FOR A CONSIDERABLE STRETCH OF ROAD, THE EYES OF THE DEAD WOULD STARE DOWN AT HIM, BEARING VACANT WITNESS TO WHAT BECAME A **SOLEMN PROCESSION** IN THEIR HONOR.
"JESUS **WELCOMED** THE SILENCE. HE KNEW IT WOULDN'T **LAST.**

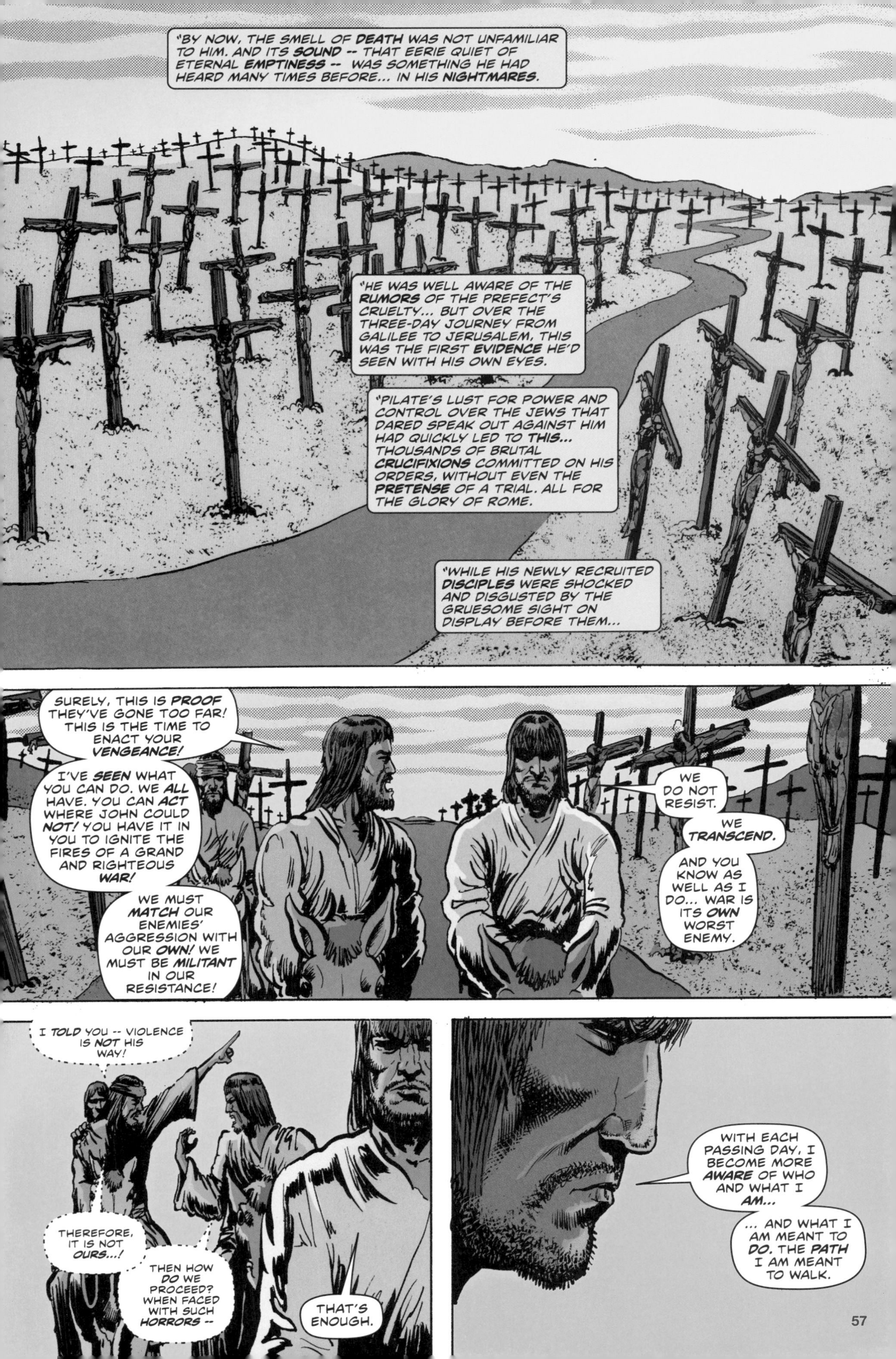
"BY NOW, THE SMELL OF DEATH WAS NOT UNFAMILIAR TO HIM. AND ITS SOUND -- THAT EERIE QUIET OF ETERNAL EMPTINESS -- WAS SOMETHING HE HAD HEARD MANY TIMES BEFORE... IN HIS NIGHTMARES.
"HE WAS WELL AWARE OF THE RUMORS OF THE PREFECT'S CRUELTY... BUT OVER THE THREE-DAY JOURNEY FROM GALILEE TO JERUSALEM, THIS WAS THE FIRST EVIDENCE HE'D SEEN WITH HIS OWN EYES.
"PILATE'S LUST FOR POWER AND CONTROL OVER THE JEWS THAT DARED SPEAK OUT AGAINST HIM HAD QUICKLY LED TO THIS... THOUSANDS OF BRUTAL CRUCIFIXIONS COMMITTED ON HIS ORDERS, WITHOUT EVEN THE PRETENSE OF A TRIAL. ALL FOR THE GLORY OF ROME.
"WHILE HIS NEWLY RECRUITED DISCIPLES WERE SHOCKED AND DISGUSTED BY THE GRUESOME SIGHT ON DISPLAY BEFORE THEM...
SURELY, THIS IS PROOF THEY'VE GONE TOO FAR! THIS IS THE TIME TO ENACT YOUR VENGEANCE!
I'VE SEEN WHAT YOU CAN DO. WE ALL HAVE. YOU CAN ACT WHERE JOHN COULD NOT! YOU HAVE IT IN YOU TO IGNITE THE FIRES OF A GRAND AND RIGHTEOUS WAR!
WE MUST MATCH OUR ENEMIES' AGGRESSION WITH OUR OWN! WE MUST BE MILITANT IN OUR RESISTANCE!
WE DO NOT RESIST.
WE TRANSCEND.
AND YOU KNOW AS WELL AS I DO... WAR IS ITS OWN WORST ENEMY.
I TOLD YOU -- VIOLENCE IS NOT HIS WAY!
THEREFORE, IT IS NOT OURS...!
THEN HOW DO WE PROCEED? WHEN FACED WITH SUCH HORRORS --
THAT'S ENOUGH.
WITH EACH PASSING DAY, I BECOME MORE AWARE OF WHO AND WHAT I AM...
... AND WHAT I AM MEANT TO DO. THE PATH I AM MEANT TO WALK.

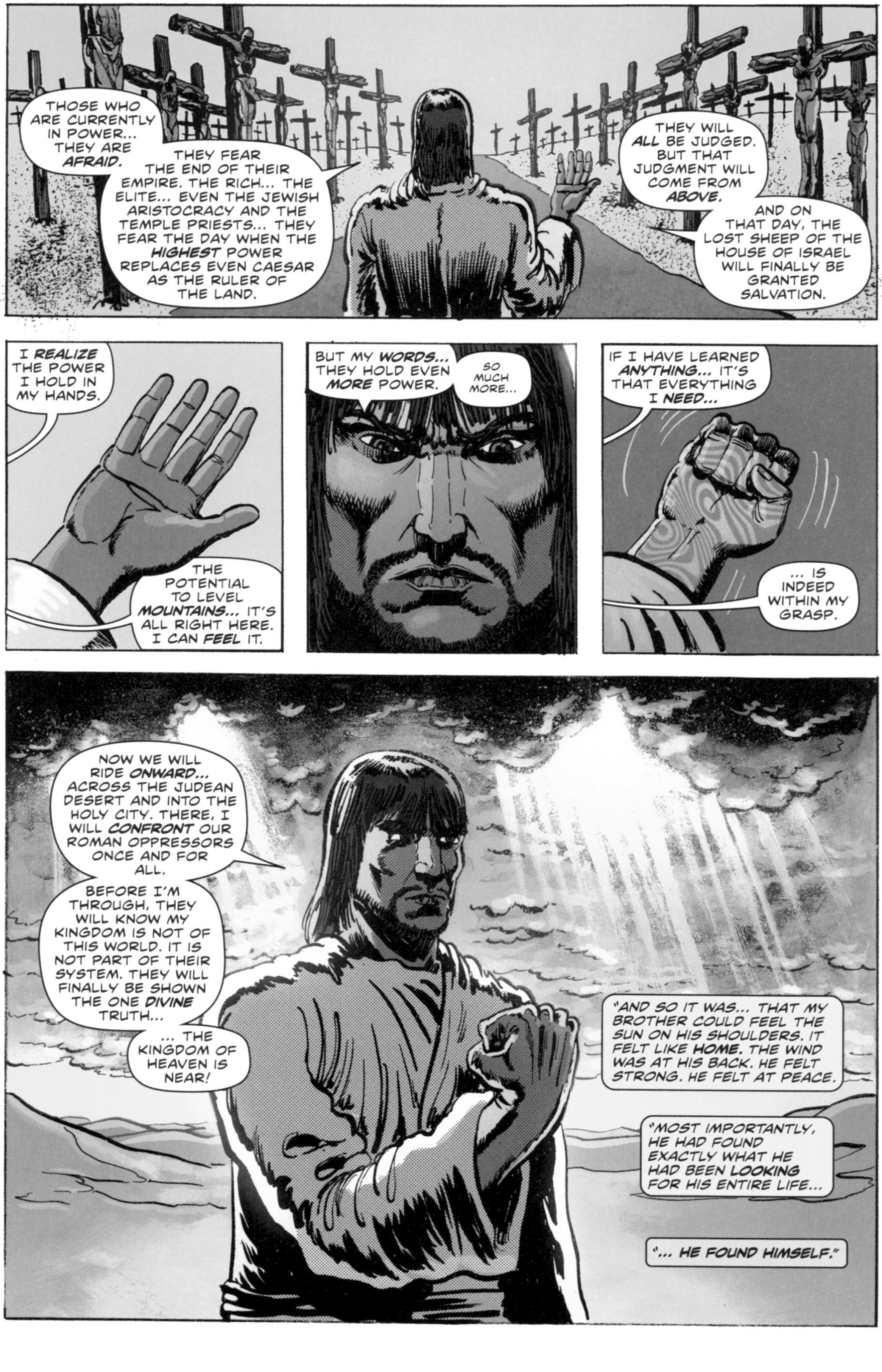
THOSE WHO ARE CURRENTLY IN POWER... THEY ARE AFRAID.
THEY FEAR THE END OF THEIR EMPIRE. THE RICH... THE ELITE... EVEN THE JEWISH ARISTOCRACY AND THE TEMPLE PRIESTS... THEY FEAR THE DAY WHEN THE HIGHEST POWER REPLACES EVEN CAESAR AS THE RULER OF THE LAND.
THEY WILL ALL BE JUDGED. BUT THAT JUDGMENT WILL COME FROM ABOVE.
AND ON THAT DAY, THE LOST SHEEP OF THE HOUSE OF ISRAEL WILL FINALLY BE GRANTED SALVATION.
I REALIZE THE POWER I HOLD IN MY HANDS.
THE POTENTIAL TO LEVEL MOUNTAINS... IT'S ALL RIGHT HERE. I CAN FEEL IT.
BUT MY WORDS... THEY HOLD EVEN MORE POWER.
SO MUCH MORE...
IF I HAVE LEARNED ANYTHING... IT'S THAT EVERYTHING I NEED...
... IS INDEED WITHIN MY GRASP.
NOW WE WILL RIDE ONWARD... ACROSS THE JUDEAN DESERT AND INTO THE HOLY CITY. THERE, I WILL CONFRONT OUR ROMAN OPPRESSORS ONCE AND FOR ALL.
BEFORE I'M THROUGH, THEY WILL KNOW MY KINGDOM IS NOT OF THIS WORLD. IT IS NOT PART OF THEIR SYSTEM. THEY WILL FINALLY BE SHOWN THE ONE DIVINE TRUTH...
... THE KINGDOM OF HEAVEN IS NEAR!
"AND SO IT WAS... THAT MY BROTHER COULD FEEL THE SUN ON HIS SHOULDERS. IT FELT LIKE HOME. THE WIND WAS AT HIS BACK. HE FELT STRONG. HE FELT AT PEACE.
"MOST IMPORTANTLY, HE HAD FOUND EXACTLY WHAT HE HAD BEEN LOOKING FOR HIS ENTIRE LIFE...
"... HE FOUND HIMSELF."

THE END

AUTHORS' NOTE

There are, invariably, a few things to say after the fact...

One of the reasons we did this book was to celebrate the pure power of comicbooks.

If this book is a testament (no pun intended) to *anything*, it's to the hard-won fact that comicbooks -- as a *medium* -- can tell any type of story. They are not -- nor should they ever be -- limited by genre, character or subject matter. Their potential is limitless.

Even now, a lot of people automatically conflate comicbooks with superheroes. Fair enough. Seen through a certain lens, that might often seem like an inescapable truth. But, as creators, *we* don't view the medium through that lens. It's far too constricting.

Some legendary creators that came before us have spent the majority of their careers proving this very point with significant work that will be remembered forever, for its artistry as much as its genre-busting qualities. Will Eisner inadvertently became the grandfather of the modern graphic novel with *A Contract With God*. Creators like Daniel Clowes, Charles Burns, Los Bros Hernandez and Chester Brown were early prophets, each in their own way. In particular, Art Spiegelman and his most famous graphic novel, *Maus*, made an enormous literary impact, even beyond the confines of comicbook culture. Similarly, the late Harvey Pekar and his *American Splendor* books were another important example of the kinds of stories that comicbooks were more than capable of telling.

Even mainstream giants knew the true value of the medium beyond the four-color spinner racks that so comfortably housed all those children's power fantasies. Alan Moore might be best known for bona fide genre classics like *Watchmen*, *Miracleman* and *Swamp Thing*, but he also contributed plenty of left-of-center works like *A Small Killing* (with Oscar Zarate), *From Hell* (with Eddie Campbell), *Lost Girls* (with Melinda Gebbie) and, most notably, the epic "Shadowplay" story in *Brought To Light* (with Bill Sienkiewicz). These were more vital examples of the medium not being permanently tied to any particular message.

There have been many others, but regardless of whether or not we've namechecked them here, these creative forebearers were spiritual inspirations for the book you now hold in your hands. They were pioneers, one and all, nobly pointing the way down a path for the rest of us to travel. They used the medium in ways that others hadn't even contemplated.

Simultaneously, we also took some obvious aesthetic inspiration from the full-on genre comicbooks of the mid-1970s. The work done at that time represents a brief window of artistic freedom that hadn't been seen since the classic EC Comics of the 1950s and has never been replicated in our industry's history (for a variety of reasons). It might've been unintentional, but that history shows it was the last gasp of mass market, newsstand comicbooks attempting to present diverse genres, other than the standard superhero fare. Kung fu, mysteries, westerns, sci fi, funny animals, war, sword and sorcery... they were all part of Marvel and DC's publishing slates. Combined with the editorial chaos that existed during that period and you ended up with some of the strangest, most bizarre comicbooks that have ever existed. And a kid could pick them up off their local newsstand for 20 cents, 30 cents, 40 cents a pop...!

Admittedly, like many adults these days (who wallow in their arrested adolescence with a vigor that is, at times, inexplicable), the mainstream comicbooks of our youth still reside deep within our hearts. To deny their impact on our work -- and this work in particular -- would be a lie. Comicbooks of any and all stripe are embedded in our DNA, and so their influence comes out in just about everything we do.

And now, many decades later...we find ourselves existing in a small but significantly stubborn marketplace where a breadth and diversity of material is readily available, and that alone owes everything to the ground that was broken by those that came before. Everything we've been through has brought us to a place where comicbooks have been accepted as a fully formed expression of artistic ambition, more than capable of mining the deepest emotions, exploring the most complex subject matter and presenting any kind of story.

Most importantly, the medium of comicbooks is about having an experience. More specifically, a very *personal* experience, one that is unique to each and every reader. In that way, it's an extremely *interactive* medium... meaning that the reader brings just as much to the party as the creators do. It's the kind of thing that separates comicbooks from just about every other storytelling medium. And, in our opinion, it's one of things that makes it the *superior* medium.

So, at the end of the day, we hope we've provided you with an experience of *some* kind, one you won't soon forget.

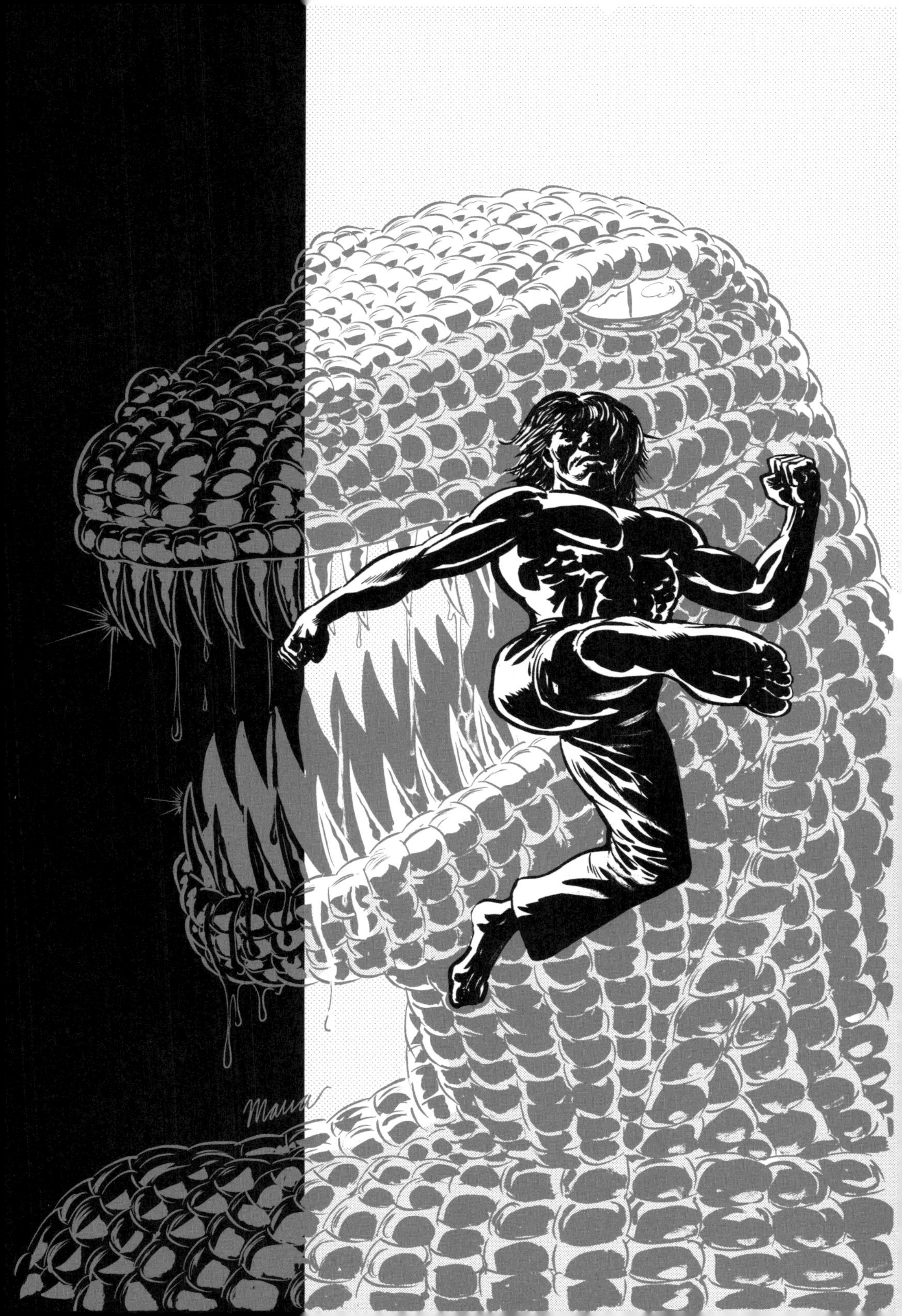

ABOUT THE CREATORS

JOE CASEY (writer) escaped a childhood filled with nothing but comicbooks, movies and rock n' roll... only to crash headlong into an adulthood filled with nothing but comicbooks, movies and rock 'n' roll. Next to bringing his own twisted offspring into the world, finding a way to get paid for his interests is his greatest personal achievement. As a founding partner in Man of Action Entertainment, he also moonlights as a writer/producer in the field of televised entertainment.

BENJAMIN MARRA (artist) is a Grammy-nominated illustrator and cartoonist. His comic-book work has been compared to mainstream legends such as Jim Steranko and Paul Gulacy, as well as underground comix heroes R. Crumb and Spain. Marra's illustrations have been recognized by The Society of Illustrators, The Society of Publication Designers and American Illustration. In 2016, Marra provided the cover art for the American Illustration Annual #35. In 2006, the Art Directors Club named Marra as one of their Young Guns. Some of his clients include adult swim, *Playboy*, *Rolling Stone*, *The New York Times*, Marvel Comics, *Vice*, *Radar*, *Paper*, *Nylon*, Wieden+Kennedy, Doubleday & Cartwright and McCann-Erickson.

BRAD SIMPSON'S (colorist) distinct color art has appeared in numerous titles including *The Amazing Spiderman*, *30 Days of Night* and in the current monthly series *Bloodborne*. He resides in Oakland, California, with his wife, Sarah, and sons, Clive and Maddox. When he is not on a deadline, he enjoys anticipating future deadlines.

SONIA HARRIS (graphic designer) is a Londoner who lives in Los Angeles. She has been designing books, patterns, ad campaigns, infographics and logos for more than two decades. She loves it. She has nothing funny to add to this, her career is probably less amusing than everyone else's here...

Find more of her design work on her site: **soyabean.com** and her swearing patterns at: **secretbean.com**

RUS WOOTON (letterer) has been lettering comics since 2003, been drawing for as long as he can remember and been reading comics for most of his life. A vagabond by circumstance and by choice, he's lived in 7 states and 21 domiciles, currently holed up in a tiny studio somewhere in Los Angeles. These days, his lettering and logos can mostly be found in and on comics published by Image. Mostly.

OTHER WORKS BY JOE CASEY

MCMLXXV
WITH IAN MACEWAN

ANNUAL
WITH LUKE PRKER & VARIOUS

NEW LIEUTENANTS OF METAL
WITH ULISES FARINAS

SEX
WITH PIOTR KOWALSKI

GØDLAND
WITH TOM SCIOLI

THE BOUNCE
WITH DAVID MESSINA & SONIA HARRIS

BUTCHER BAKER THE RIGHTEOUS MAKER
WITH MIKE HUDDLESTON

VALHALLA MAD
WITH PAUL MAYBURY

CODEFLESH
WITH CHARLIE ADLARD

OFFICER DOWNE
WITH CHRIS BURNHAM

ROCK BOTTOM
WITH CHARLIE ADLARD

NIXON'S PALS
WITH CHRIS BURNHAM

CHARLATAN BALL
WITH ANDY SURIANO

DOC BIZARRE, M.D.
WITH ANDY SURIANO

THE MILKMAN MURDERS
WITH STEVE PARKHOUSE

FULL MOON FEVER
WITH CALEB GERARD/DAMIAN COUCEIRO

KRASH BASTARDS
WITH AXEL 13

OTHER WORKS BY BENJAMIN MARRA

TERROR ASSAULTER: O.M.W.O.T.
[ONE MAN WAR ON TERROR]

AMERICAN BLOOD

NIGHT BUSINESS

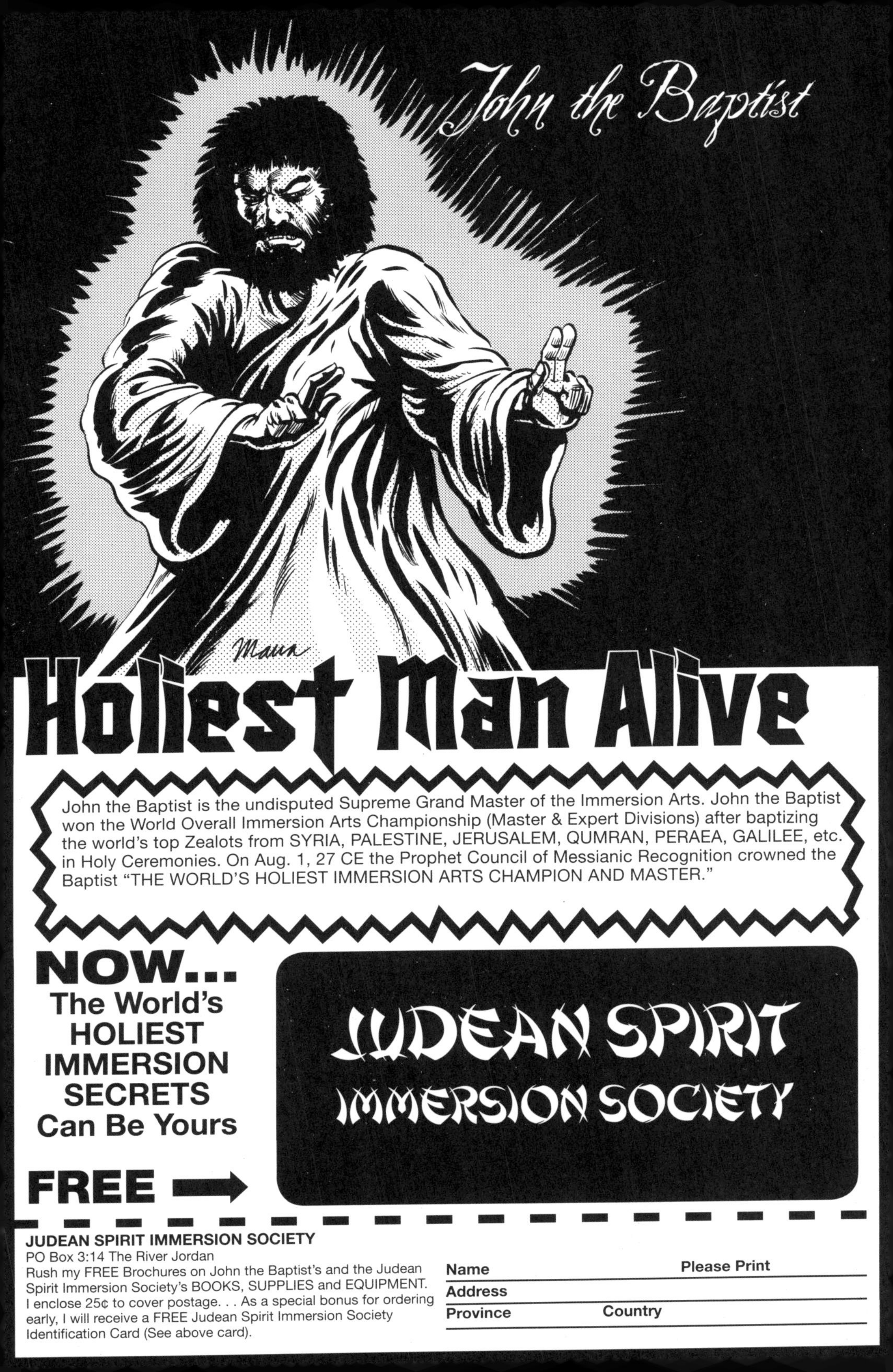
John the Baptist
Holiest Man Alive
John the Baptist is the undisputed Supreme Grand Master of the Immersion Arts. John the Baptist won the World Overall Immersion Arts Championship (Master & Expert Divisions) after baptizing the world's top Zealots from SYRIA, PALESTINE, JERUSALEM, QUMRAN, PERAEA, GALILEE, etc. in Holy Ceremonies. On Aug. 1, 27 CE the Prophet Council of Messianic Recognition crowned the Baptist "THE WORLD'S HOLIEST IMMERSION ARTS CHAMPION AND MASTER."
NOW...
The World's HOLIEST IMMERSION SECRETS Can Be Yours
FREE
JUDEAN SPIRIT IMMERSION SOCIETY
JUDEAN SPIRIT IMMERSION SOCIETY
PO Box 3:14 The River Jordan
Rush my FREE Brochures on John the Baptist's and the Judean Spirit Immersion Society's BOOKS, SUPPLIES and EQUIPMENT. I enclose 25¢ to cover postage. . . As a special bonus for ordering early, I will receive a FREE Judean Spirit Immersion Society Identification Card (See above card).
Name
Please Print
Address
Province
Country

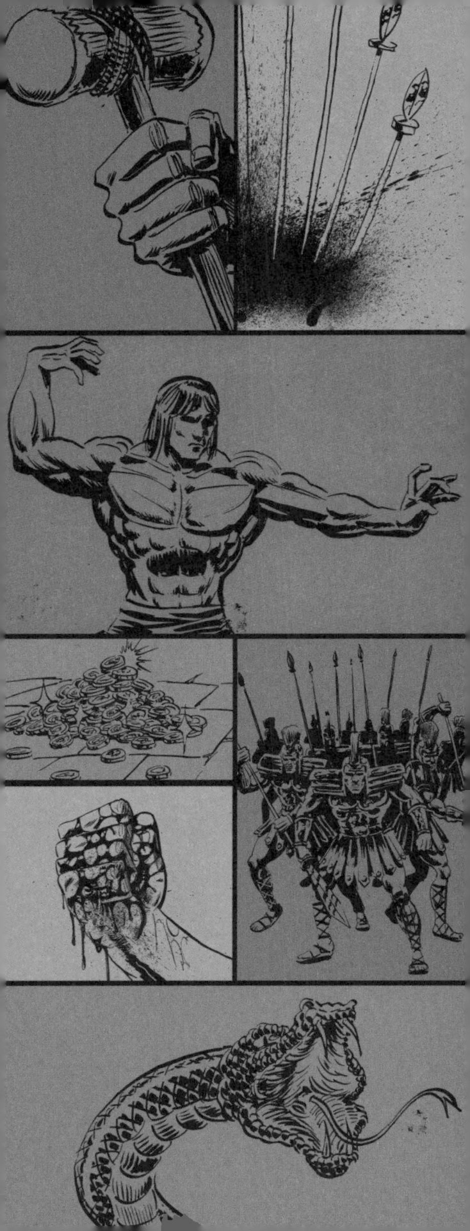

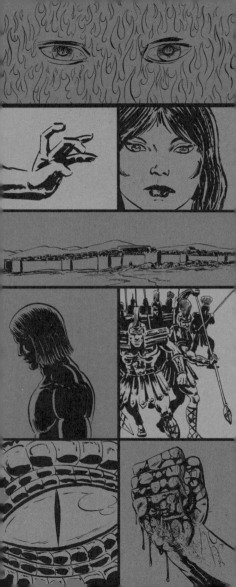

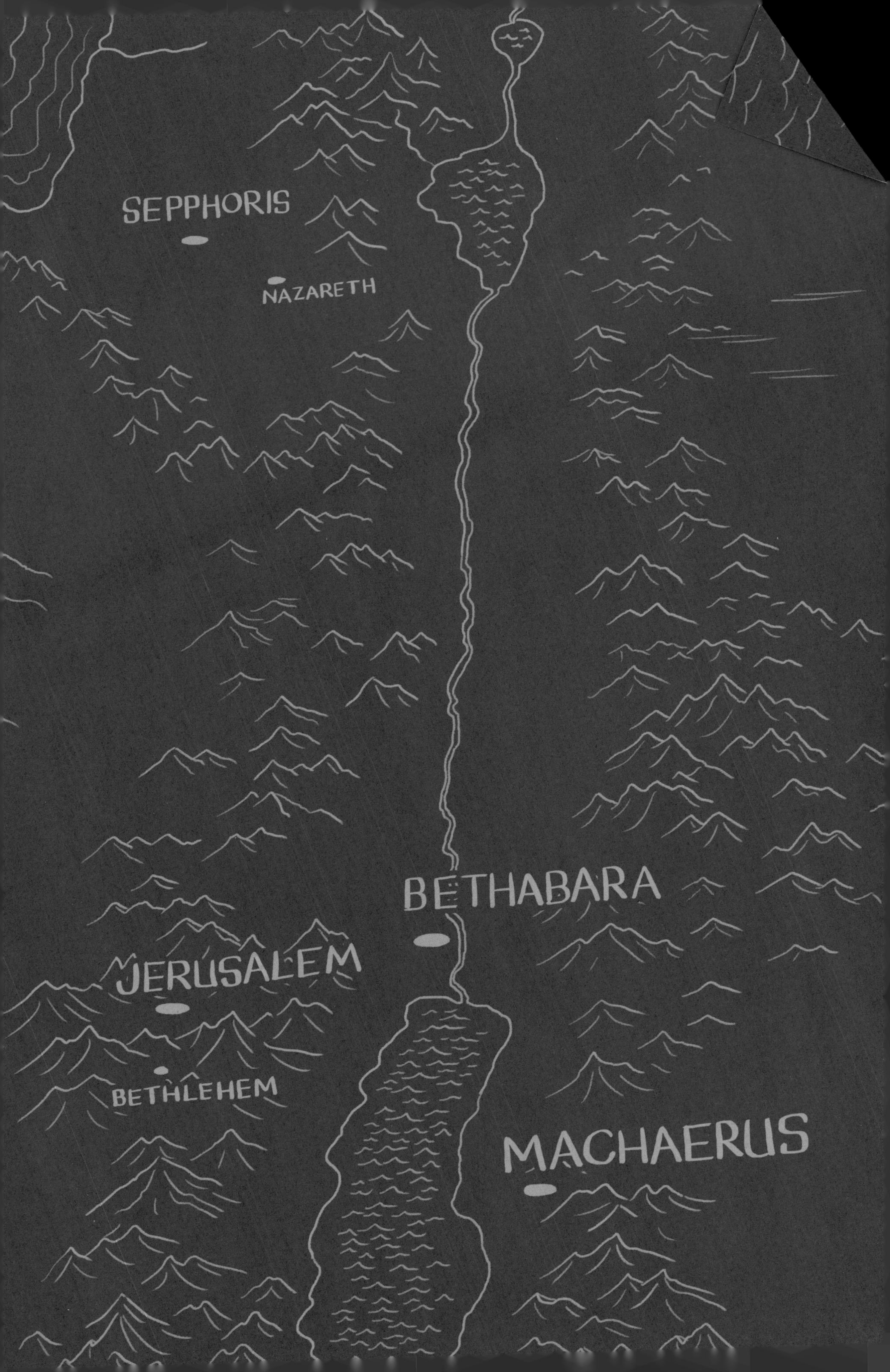
SEPPHORIS
NAZARETH
BETHABARA
JERUSALEM
BETHLEHEM
MACHAERUS

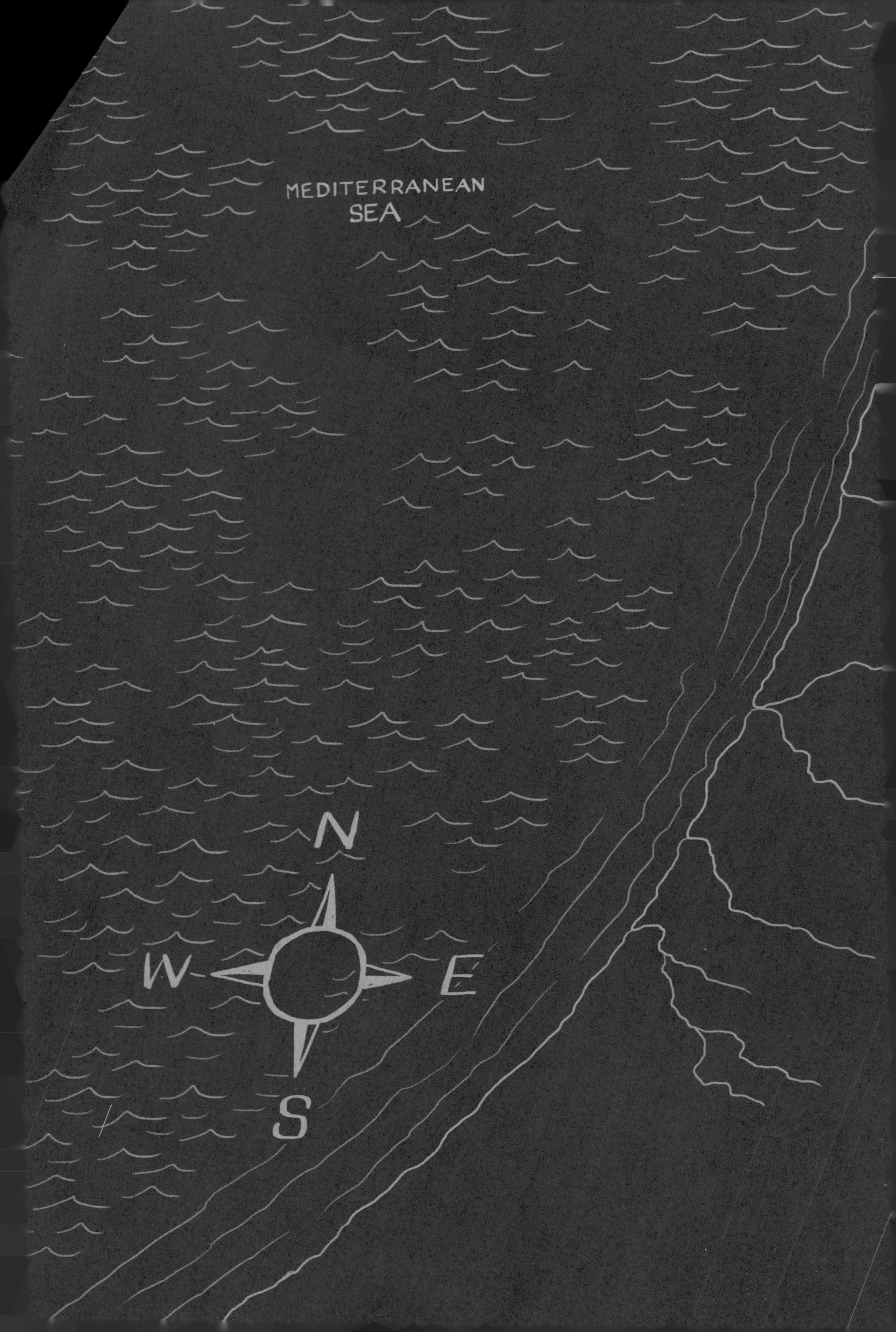
MEDITERRANEAN
SEA
N
W
E
S